TIMELESS

Magic City

By R. Earl Muir

TIMELESS

Magic City

By R. Earl Muir

First Edition
First Printing, 2022

Book Design by Robert Patterson
Cover Design by REBOB Art
Cover Art by Mara Jambor
Final Cover Design and Production by Anna Harmon
Edited by Michael Perez
and Dr. Jesse R. Hale, PhD

ISBIN: 979-8-9868434-4-5

TIMELESS

Magic City

By R. Earl Muir

ACKNOWLEDGEMENTS

This is a work of fiction, but many of the references made to actual landmarks, historical persons, and historical events are presented to the best of the author's knowledge and ability.

The characters and the story are strictly fictional and a product of the author's imagination. Any names, characters, businesses, places, events, locales, and incidents are either the products of the author's imagination or used in a fictitious manner. Any resemblance to actual persons, living or dead, or actual places or events is purely coincidental.

My research for this book was made much easier by BHAMWIKI and to all those who create, contribute to, and maintain this excellent website, and I am eternally grateful.

I am indebted to a number of people whose contributions to this book are invaluable. My wife and biggest cheerleader in life, Pam Patterson, Randy Hale, Sandy Herren, and Mike Perez all served as friends and counsel, as well as proofreaders, editors, and moral support throughout the process. I could not have done it without them.

Also, a rough draft of this project was sent out to a few friends and readers early on for feedback. Thanks to Mark Ritter and David Henderson for your honest feedback that helped this book get off the ground.

Finally, I must thank our great city of Birmingham and my fellow citizens. The rich history, both good and bad, of the Magic City offers a complex and compelling backdrop for the stories banging around in my head. I have been privileged to travel the world, but I cannot imagine living anywhere else.

Harvey Alexander Patterson
11/27/2009 – 05/23/2022

DEDICATION

This book is dedicated to my faithful companion, co-author, playmate, and giver of unconditional love for the last thirteen years, Harvey Alexander Patterson.

We've had dogs all our lives and each and every one has been special, and we hold a place in our hearts for each of them, but something about that dappled, twenty-pound dachshund was different. Maybe it was my age of wisdom and reflection, maybe it was his personality, or a combination of both, but he was truly a companion and so much more.

He was stubborn like most of his breed and was absolutely sure he was a Doberman. If you ever met him, he was not a friendly dog. He would bark and growl at you or ignore you. If he didn't, then you too were very special. He considered a handful of people as friends, and I feel privileged to have been one. To his brother who predeceased him by a few years, he was a rock solid loving companion but to most other dogs, he was aloof, at best, usually turning away as though they were not worthy of breathing his same air. But to us, he was the most loving and demonstrative dog we have ever had the pleasure of knowing.

He loved to cuddle close. He loved a toy more than any dog we have ever known and loved to get a new one even more. Like a child on Christmas morning, nothing brought him more joy than a new toy. Some he only played with for a minute. Some he would wear out and we had "back-ups" to slip in when they got so worn.

As I wrote my first novels and as I churned out my monthly magazine articles, he was a constant companion through every step. He was with me through this book too. Either laying at my feet under the desk, or curled up in the chair just behind me, he was there and now that he is not, I miss him.

He lived a great life, and I cannot be really sad because his memories continue to bring me joy and remind me to live each moment of every day to the fullest. Thanks, Harvey for sharing your life with me and being the best writing companion I could ever dream of having.

PREFACE

As a life-long resident of Birmingham, Alabama, the city's rich and troubled history has always intrigued me. From its humble origins just after the Civil War to its rapid ascension as a center of industry and economic development in the early twentieth century that gave the city the title of the Magic City and into the next century as a symbol of human rights and a progressive city with a world class medical center, Birmingham has been a complex place to live and work. The ebb and flow through the decades have gripped my attention and imagination since childhood and continue to do so now.

My first two novels, *Magic City Murder Déjà Vu and BOMBINGHAM A Day of Reckoning*, were modern day crime stories with a heavy dose of Birmingham history. This book follows that same path but with a big difference as most of the story takes place in the first decade of the twentieth century as Birmingham was transforming from a young, booming mining town into a city drawing worldwide attention for its industrial and economic prowess.

I have always been fascinated with this time period and particularly in regard to my hometown as skyscrapers began to emerge throughout the city as the mines and steel mills boomed. Immigrants from around the world flooded in to take advantage of the opportunities here. During the building boom of that decade, four buildings would rise on the corners of 1st Avenue North and

20th Street. This would be referred to in a magazine article at the time as the heaviest corner in the south. That distinction would soon grow in reputation as "the heaviest corner on earth" as Birmingham was recognized as a modern city with unlimited potential. Those four buildings stand today either renovated and repurposed or renovations are underway, and the moniker of "Heaviest Corner" is still widely used.

As I researched my previous novels, I was also struck by how similar our social issues were more than a hundred years removed --- immigration, race, religion, and politics seemed to run similar paths both then and now. This book delves into those social issues and all that has changed and all that has unfortunately not changed enough.

My hope is that the fictional story portrayed in this book is entertaining but also educational in reminding us that we need to relish our relationships. Time is never guaranteed and while many things come and go, it is our relationships that endure and impact generations to come.

Chapter 1

Sam Robbins was still adjusting to his new life. After twenty-five years with the Birmingham Police Department (BPD) and twelve more with the U.S. Marshal Service, he pulled the pin for good two weeks ago and was settling into his new life as a retiree -- a life without cases to solve or bad guys to chase. He was even getting used to leaving his gun at home. He rarely even thought about it except when he got dressed every morning. A sidearm had been a part of his wardrobe for almost forty years so it was a weird feeling to not carry it. He had retired before, but he hoped this one was going to stick. The official retirement date was the end of the year, but the party was over, and his office cleaned out. He was getting used to retirement life while burning vacation and PTO accumulated over the last twelve years of working overtime on countless investigations. He was finally ready to slow down and just enjoy life.

He applied for his retirement from the police department as soon as he had his twenty-five years in, but since he was only forty-six at the time, he knew he wasn't going to hit the rocking chair just yet. His wife, Joan, was a schoolteacher and was also eligible for retirement after twenty-five years so they both took their retirement and went on a two-week vacation before each started their new careers. His as a Deputy U.S. Marshal in the Birmingham office of the Northern Alabama District and hers at the University of Alabama at Birmingham, as a Professor in the History Department.

Joan had enjoyed her years as a high school teacher in the Birmingham School system but soon after she and Sam married, she resumed her studies in the evening and summers earning two master's degrees and eventually her PhD, all while being a dedicated teacher to some of the most vulnerable students in the inner city.

Sam had long grown tired of the bureaucracy of the police department. He had risen to the rank of Lieutenant having served stints in the Patrol, Tactical, and Detectives divisions. His last fourteen years had been spent in the Homicide Division. Although he had worked a few who-done-it's in his career, most of the homicides in Birmingham were like most homicides in cities anywhere in the U.S. They involved some low life hoodlum who had no value of his own life, much less others, so a gun was his method of conflict resolution and it never ended well. The conflicts usually involved someone disrespecting someone else over a car, or a woman, or drugs, or something trivial. Working the cases day in and day out just wore you down and after twenty-five years, he was ready to move on. Even with a stellar record of closing cases, it seemed futile in a city with a per capita murder rate that consistently landed in the top ten in the country.

When his long-time friend, Mac Johnson, was appointed the U.S. Marshal of the Northern Alabama District, he began to recruit Sam to join his staff. Two years later he had completed his years with BPD and submitted his retirement papers and called Mac. The day his retirement from the police department was official, he was sworn in as a Deputy U.S. Marshal.

2

When the title of U. S. Marshal is mentioned, most people think about Wyatt Earp, cowboy movies, and TV shows set in the wild west. The service certainly played a key role as western territories needed law and order as the country expanded, but the service is much more than that. In its long history there have been both good and bad aspects as the service was often required to fulfill a duty to the conscious of the nation at the time. Sometimes it was good and noble and sometimes the duty was horrific, especially viewed in the eyes of history.

The U.S. Marshal Service is oldest law enforcement agency in the U.S. created by Congress in 1789 and signed into law by President Washington who appointed the first thirteen Marshals, one to each state.

In 1850, the Fugitive Slave Act was passed by Congress and Marshals were tasked with arresting and returning fugitive slaves to their masters until 1861 when the Civil War began and their duties changed drastically. That same year, the service became the forerunner of the Secret Service when U.S. Marshal Ward Hill Lamon became the bodyguard of President Lincoln at his inauguration. The President continually objected to Lamon's overzealous efforts to protect him and when the President was assassinated on April 14, 1865, Lamon was on an assignment out of the district leaving the President's protection in the hands of local police.

During the war, not only did the Marshals abandon chasing runaway slaves, but they also sought out Confederate spies and confiscated property used in support of the Confederacy.

In the decades leading up to prohibition, Marshals assisted IRS Agents in enforcing whiskey tax laws.

During World War I while American troops were fighting in Europe, the service protected the home front from enemy spies and saboteurs.

During the Civil Rights era of the 1960's, the service was often called on to keep order and enforce laws. U.S. Marshals escorted the child, Ruby Bridges, to her elementary school in New Orleans as integration began. Teams of Marshals were assigned to protect James Meredith at the University of Mississippi around the clock until his graduation. One year later, Alabama Governor George Wallace, defying a federal court order, orchestrated the media event of standing in the doorway of Foster Auditorium on the campus of the University of Alabama to defy enrollment to two African American students. The students were escorted past Wallace after President Kennedy federalized the Alabama National Guard. Backed by the guard, the students were escorted in by Marshals.

Today the U.S. Marshal Service performs a variety of duties including witness security, fugitive apprehension, serving federal court documents and working special investigations with the Federal Prosecutors in the Department of Justice and that was why Sam was recruited by Mac to join his team. Most of Sam's police career was spent investigating everything from terror plots to corrupt politicians and Mac knew he would be an asset in the Birmingham office.

It had been a nice turn from the daily grind as a city detective, but at fifty-eight years old, Sam was now ready to leave his gun at home and be a normal citizen for the first time in his adult life. When he took the job, he promised Mac ten years and no more. He and Joan planned to travel and enjoy life before they got too old to do so. But two years before the couple's planned escape, Joan was diagnosed with an aggressive form of breast cancer and was gone in nine months' time. Sam was devastated and did the only thing he knew to do --- he threw himself into his work. But now, after four years of non-stop grind, he was finally ready. He still missed Joan every day and knew he would for the rest of his life. They never had kids and had been each other's constant companion and best friend since high school. Sam knew that he was lost without Joan and tried not to spiral into depression. Although he had support from friends, he knew that the only thing that would save him was getting lost in work. So, instead of that planned retirement, he immersed himself back in the job, but now seemed like the time to finally emerge and try his hand at a normal life.

After Joan's death, Sam sold their suburban home and moved into a loft in the city, something they had talked for years about doing. He credited that move with saving his sanity, if not his life. He had met a vibrant group of empty nesters living downtown and had as much of a social life as he wanted. Some days he stayed in and read and listened to music but other times he joined a group of his neighbors to go to plays, concerts, or just an evening meal or cocktails.

After two weeks as a man of leisure he had begun to settle into a new routine, but today would prove to be anything but routine.

He would usually leave the loft for a light breakfast at one of the many options in his neighborhood and then walk around the city for exercise. It was October, so the morning walks were pleasant. He knew when the brief winter arrived, he would have to move his exercise to the warmer afternoon and once the long summer arrived, he would have to either do it in the early morning or evening to escape the brutal heat of an Alabama summer that one must experience to fully understand. But for now, this routine was perfect. He usually made his way down Morris Avenue from the rear of his loft and once he reached the center of the city went either left to the southside, right to the northside, or kept straight for a few blocks and ended up at Railroad Park where he would take a stroll around the park and then head home via the Rotary Trail.

Railroad Park is a seventeen-acre oasis nestled between 14th and 18th Streets, along 1st Avenue South in the center of the city. The old, abandoned rail yard was converted into an urban park in 2010, and soon developments began to spring up all around it. First, the minor league baseball park, Regions Field, was built just across 1st Avenue South and soon the vacant warehouses and buildings in the surrounding blocks began transformation into lofts, apartments, restaurants, bars, and social gathering hubs. The area is now designated as the Parkside District and is flourishing with activity day and night.

Rotary Trail, originally called Line Park before the local Rotary Club stepped in to fund most of the project, is a linear park space that runs where an abandoned rail line once ran through the center of the city. It serves as a median in the center of 1st Avenue South from 20th Street eastward. The trail extended to 24th street in the initial phase and with the most recent extension now goes to 41st Street in the trendy Avondale neighborhood. The space is marked by a large replica of the "Birmingham -- The Magic City" sign that once stood to greet travelers departing the old Terminal Rail Station in downtown. The new LED lighted sign spans the trail as it begins at the intersection of 20th Street and is a photo-op for locals as well as visitors to the city. The trail drops below grade as it moves eastward through downtown and even though it is in the center of the city, the lush plantings and quiet peace provide an escape for a brief moment. The original space provides a four-block refuge from the normal walk along city streets before emerging back on grade under the Red Mountain Expressway. Sam took the route at least twice a week on his walks.

Sam had started the daily routine to make sure he didn't end up secluded in the loft all day doing nothing, something he quietly feared since his work routine was such a part of his very being. Retirement was a little frightening for him. Especially without Joan. His work routine was now over, but he still needed a routine, so he walked and got in his exercise before heading back home for a shower and then getting lunch. He often met with some of his friends or just made a quick lunch at the loft. For almost two weeks the new routine seemed to be working. He only missed work a couple of times and quickly found something else to do to occupy his mind.

After moving downtown, he had begun to paint again as a hobby. At first it was the resumption of a lifelong pastime but then his friends convinced him to show his art at the monthly Art Crawl event downtown and he sold a few. He now showed at art shows in town a few times a year. It was still just a hobby to him and mostly a way of forced relaxation from a high-pressure job and now a way to stave off boredom in retirement. He usually spent at least a couple of hours in the afternoon painting before meeting friends for cocktails and sometimes dinner. There were so many great options within a four-block walk. After dinner, he would head back to the loft and spin some tunes from his expansive record collection and read or watch TV until he got ready for bed. It was a routine, but it also included enough variety to ensure that it could last and not get too boring. He was ready to try retirement, but knew he had to stay busy. So far, so good, but he was only two weeks in.

Today the weather was almost perfect. A rarity in Alabama where the mild winters are short lived, and the prolonged hot summers rarely offer a transition of autumn or spring. Today was very pleasant as Sam started on his journey after a breakfast croissant and a tall coffee at June Coffee on 25th. From the coffee shop, he travelled south to Morris Avenue and then turned right onto Morris. This morning he planned to turn right when he reached 18th street and make his way over to Oak Hill Cemetery where most of the city's founders and elite were buried.

The historic cemetery is owned and maintained by the city and now stands adjacent to the Birmingham-Jefferson Civic Complex and nearby Protective Stadium, Uptown Entertainment District, and CityWalk Park. Sam loved his walks there and took this route at least once a week. He loved the solitude of the sprawling old cemetery, the final resting place for so many

8

amidst the hustle and bustle of the convention center, hotels, and freeways that now surround it. Could the city founders buried there have imagined the city as it is today?

As Sam turned off 25th Street onto Morris, he remembered to click the walk app on his iWatch to record his exercise and picked up his pace. After multiple knee surgeries from high school sports and a bullet that landed just above the right knee a few years ago, a fast pace for Sam was more of an uninterrupted brisk walk than it was a true speed walk, but it was better than nothing and was pretty much the only exercise he got these days.

Sam passed the back of his loft building near 24th street and waved to a neighbor in a BMW that was emerging from the garage door as he passed. As he walked under the concrete overpass of 24th Street the temp dropped slightly in the darkness under the bridge overhead. He noticed a large boxed wedged on the ledge under the bridge on his right. The spot was a favorite temporary residence for the homeless population although the police moved them along before they could get too settled.

Bridges built in the early 1900's ran from 1st Avenue North to 2nd Avenue South on 24th, 22nd, and 21st Street, now known as Richard Arrington Jr. Boulevard in honor of the city's first black Mayor. The bridges spanned the old Morris and Powell Avenues that were the original streets of the city and the adjacent railroad reservation that accommodates dozens of tracks that have coursed through the city for more than a hundred and fifty years. These bridges, or viaducts, were the connection between the city's southside and its sprawling medical center and UAB Campus and the city's northside that was home to the financial district, corporate headquarters, tech companies and the convention complex. In the early days of the city, it was hard to travel between the north and south sides due to the number of tracks and frequency of trains traveling through the city, so the viaducts and later underpasses created an unfettered connection.

At the intersection of 23rd Street the narrow Morris Avenue got even narrower as it shrunk to the original 1870 width and converted to one-way traffic, although cars were few and far between since the original cobblestone pavement was still present and uncovered. It is a quaint look and a great backdrop for photos and movie shoots, but the rough street was hell on modern cars.

Sam moved over to the sidewalk. The last thing he needed was to twist an ankle. It was just before nine, so the shops and offices were all still dark and quiet as he walked past. As he entered the shadow of the aging concrete of the 22nd Street overpass he felt the temp drop again. On the other side he could see the sunlight beginning to reflect off the damp brown cobblestones as the morning sun peaked over the tops of the three and four-story buildings behind him. As he emerged back into the light, he checked his watch to make sure his exercise was being recorded.

Just ahead was the last of the viaducts on his morning walk. The Rainbow Viaduct, or 21st Street viaduct, was the completed in 1918 and was dedicated on May 19, 1919, to honor the veterans of the 167th Infantry Company who fought as part of the Rainbow Division in World War I. At the center of the bridge a small plaque topped with ornamental iron eagles marking the dedication to the soldiers. The iron eagles replaced the original pair of concrete ones in 2012 that had deteriorated with a century of exposure to the wind and rain. The wide bridge above accommodated four travel lanes and parallel parking spaces on either side. It was an engineering marvel in 1919 and a bit overbuilt for the traffic at that time. Last year as plans were still developing to replace the aging structure, the city had to block it off to vehicular traffic after trucks and other heavy vehicles ignored the weight limit signs hastened the deterioration of the structure. Engineers feared not only the disaster of the bridge collapsing but doing so on the tracks below would halt interstate commerce for most of the eastern United States. With barricades at either end, the old bridge had become a favorite space for skate boarders and family strolls.

As Sam entered the damp shadow of the bridge something caught his eye to the right. A rusted door stood ajar. He had traveled this path thousands of times but had never noticed the door and wondered where it led. There were some doors on the southside of the viaducts. These doors led to stairwells that provided passage up to 1st Avenue South or down to the Rotary Trail, but he had never noticed anything on the north side.

As he came to the door his paced slowed and his curiosity commanded that he investigate, so he carefully pulled the door open to peer inside. All he could see was blackness. He stepped back and looked at the rusty steel door again. *Why have I never noticed this?* He looked up at the steel and concrete above and wondered where the stairs terminated, if it was indeed a stairwell. He had also walked and driven over the viaduct thousands of times. He was sure there was no door up there or stairwell.

He reached in the back pocket of his jeans and retrieved his iPhone and found the flashlight app and clicked it on. He pulled the rusty door open as far as he could and but could still see nothing in the black void. He shined the light inside, but it only reflected blackness. He slowly stepped in and suddenly was met with an intense light that blinded him. Startled, he tried to back out the door but his back hit something solid. He was blinded by the powerful light and felt the temperature plummet. Not just the coolness of the morning shadows, but extreme cold. He fumbled to find the door and then everything began to spin. He panicked. Sightless, he began feeling for the door as his years of training tried to maintain calmness amidst the growing anxiety. He had only taken a step inside the doorway but now his hands could only feel cold solid surface and he groped for something... anything to get him out of there. He felt lightheaded as he leaned on the cold surface and looked at his phone in his left hand. The screen was filled with only gray static as he pushed the button frantically. He could sense himself losing consciousness. A feeling he had only felt once when a .44 caliber slug tore into his right leg. A feeling he did not want to experience again but here it was. He felt the wave of nausea. He felt himself sliding down the wall as all went black. Black and cold as he felt his body land on the hard ground, but the cold had lessened as he fought to stay conscious. It was futile. Sam had no idea what was happening, but he knew it wasn't good. He instinctively reached for his Glock with his right hand, but only found the leather belt and remembered he was no longer carrying his weapon. It was his last thought as the darkness came.

Chapter 2

Sam was still groggy as his eyes opened. He was no longer cold, and he found himself looking up at a starry sky and a beautiful full moon. His vision was blurry, and his head was pounding. There were odd smells wafting in the air, and he wasn't sure where he was or how he got there but he was outside and that was good. He was lying on his back, and he tried to get up but found he had no strength. Lying on the ground he scanned his surroundings, but his distorted vision didn't reveal much. He rubbed his eyes and tried to focus. His years of police training made him more than a little apprehensive. As his vision began to clear it was dark, but the bright moonlight illuminated his surroundings enough for him to see. *How long have I been out? Why has no one found me? I must call for help.* He raised his left hand, but his phone was no longer there. Instead, his hand was grasping a silver pocket watch he had never seen before. He tried again to get up but was too weak. He turned his head and found himself looking down a cobblestone street. *Am I still on Morris?* Nothing looked familiar. He blinked his eyes again and could see buildings lining the street, but all was quiet. No cars or people in sight. His body was racked with pain as he turned his head in the opposite direction. He was lying in the middle of the street! His mind was racing. He tried to remember what happened but could only remember going into the doorway. *Bright light. Cold.* But that was before nine in the morning. It was clearly nighttime now. *Have I been lying here all day? Where is everyone?*

He looked again down the cobblestone street and turned to look back the other way... *not Morris! There are no overpasses.* The street stretched as far as he could see in both directions. The old buildings looked familiar, but something was off. He summoned all his strength and forced his aching body into a sitting position and the effort was like running a mile, not that he had done that in recent history, but he sat on the hard street and tried again to catch his breath.

The moon reflected softly on the damp cobblestones as he sat there trying to figure out where he was and how he got there. He was looking at his long legs splayed out as he tried to regain his strength enough to try to stand. His brain was foggy. *I must have hit my head... a concussion maybe.* He instinctively reached up to feel his head. No wounds or bumps that he could feel. Then he noticed something very odd as he sat staring at his feet. His bright green Nike running shoes had been replaced by worn leather boots. He rubbed his eyes again. His jeans were gone too! He now wore dark woolen trousers. He looked down at his chest to see the Allman Brothers Band tee shirt he had been wearing was now an off-white cotton shirt with buttons and the UAB hoodie he wore was now a black suit jacket. *I must be dreaming or hallucinating,* he thought as he carefully reexamined his wardrobe. *I have got to wake up! This is some crazy shit!*

Sam once again turned his attention to his surroundings as he scanned the buildings around him. His eyesight was improving as his eyes adjusted to the dim unlit street. He remembered the blinding light. *That's why I'm having trouble seeing! Whatever happened, must have affected my vision.* The blurriness began to clear as he scanned the street again but saw no signs of life. He tried to get his legs under him to stand but was still too weak, so he sat and scanned. A few buildings down he saw a large door was propped open. It was a garage door but not a roll-up. It was swung open like a regular door but was at least ten feet wide. It looked odd with its panel protruding to the edge of the cobblestone street. There was a flickering glow in the building, like a fireplace but he couldn't see in from this angle. He gathered his energy again determined to stand as he placed his hands on the street for leverage and once again discovered the pocket watch in his hand. He stuffed the watch in his vest pocket. *I am wearing a vest? I have got to wake up!* As Sam placed his palms on the cobblestones to try and push himself upward a voice resonating from the darkness behind him sent his heart racing again as he spun around on the street.

"You alright, Mister?" the baritone voice rang out from somewhere behind him and sent him stumbling back onto the street as he tried to find the source.

"Oh, I am so sorry Masta, I's didn't mean to scare ya," the young black man said removing his wide breamed hat and bowing his head slightly. The muscular man appeared to be in his mid-twenties and clad in baggy jeans and a heavy leather apron.

"Where am I?" Sam asked as he tried to catch his breath again, sitting on the street looking up at the imposing figure with a kind face.

17

"Youse in Burminham, Alabama, sir," the man answered as he replaced his hat but maintained a distance of several feet. He smiled gently as Sam sat there more confused than ever. "I's jest finishin' up some work over yonder and I seen you stumble," he offered pointing to the open door Sam had seen. Sam noticed then the faded, hand-painted sign above the door - ***Joseph Horton, Blacksmith and Livery***.

Sam mustered all his energy and finally stood, although somewhat wobbly at first. He glanced around again and looked at the young man standing now about six feet from him. His dark skin glistened with sweat in the moonlight, even though the night air was chilly. He stood there straight, his biceps bulging. He was just less than six feet tall and built like an NFL running back.

Sam finally felt steady on his feet, although still not sure what kind of weird dream or psychosis he was experiencing and greeted the man.

"My name is Sam," he said extending his hand as he stepped toward the blacksmith, "Sam Robbins."

The young man didn't move but seemed fixated on Sam's outstretched hand. He then nervously glanced around before extending his own to grasp Sam's in a handshake.

"I am James... James Lewis. I work yonder at the blacksmith shop. I work for Mr. Horton and his sons."

"James, it's a pleasure to meet you. Would you happen to know the date?"

"It is the 28th of October," he smiled again, "three days to payday," he beamed.

Sam's brain was racing as the cobwebs seemed to be clearing. It was the same day, so it was only a few hours he couldn't remember. But given his surroundings and his current state of dress, he had to ask.

"This is going to sound a bit crazy, but I am not thinking too clearly... what year is it?" Sam asked cautiously.

"It is 1901," James said as his smile disappeared seeing the look of fear and confusion on Sam's face. "You gon' be alright, Mister Sam?"

"Yea, I'm okay," Sam answered though clearly, he was anything but okay. "I think I may have hit my head or something. I need a place to stay. Is there somewhere near here?"

"Yes, Sir," James answered pointing down Morris, "The Metropolitan Hotel is right up yonder on 20th street by da train station. Finest in the city. It jest opened back up a week ago. Boiler blew up 'bout a year ago... whole place burned down and the buildin' next door too. They saved the train station though. Built dat hotel back fast!"

"Thanks," Sam said looking down Morris to the hotel a block away.

Sam's mind was racing as he made his way to the sidewalk and headed west toward the hotel. As he walked, his body still ached but his strength was returning. He looked at the buildings he passed. Some were familiar from his many walks through the city, others were not. He still wasn't sure what was going on, but his mind was clearing, and he wasn't sure if this was some ultra-real dream or some serious effect of a brain injury, but everything around him pointed to his hometown in 1901.

He had read enough about the city's history and architecture and Joan had somewhat of an obsession with it that had led her to not only teach classes about it, but she had also led historic tours through downtown. Sam had joined her several times although he wasn't paying close attention most of the time. As he walked and contemplated the events and his surroundings, he was sure his vague knowledge was fueling whatever this was.

As he passed the open door of the blacksmith shop, he peered in to see a small flame burning in a large cast iron surround near a large anvil and a small wooden table with other tools. A lantern hung over the table. Two large horses stood in a stall on the opposite side of the building. As he passed, he glanced back to see James going inside. He stopped and tipped his hat again before disappearing through the door.

Sam was looking at his surroundings and trying to place where he was and what things looked like before this bizarre transformation. He stared ahead at his destination, the Metropolitan Hotel, just across 20th Street. He had certainly never seen that before. The beautiful building stood on the northwest corner of Morris and 20th street and although he had walked and driven through the intersection thousands of times, he couldn't remember what was there. He knew the Woodward Building was on the corner of 1st but couldn't picture what was behind it. Nothing remarkable, he was sure. *Maybe a parking deck?* The large five-story hotel was stunning and looked brand new and according to James it was. He stopped in a dark shadow near the corner and stared at the hotel. On the south side of Morris across from the hotel, he saw two men emerge from the building. They were too far away to see clearly in the dim light, but both wore flat top caps and uniform jackets. *Railroad employees! Probably conductors. The Terminal Station wasn't completed until 1909, so this was the main station in 1901. I think it was called Union Station or was it the L & N?*

Sam remembered the watch he put in his pocket and pulled it out -- twenty past nine. He had lost about twelve hours of time, not counting the one hundred twenty-one years. He searched his trouser pockets for his wallet and pulled out a wad of neatly folded cash. He remembered he had stopped by the ATM to get cash for the contractor coming tomorrow to install a new kitchen sink in his loft. He looked around to ensure he was still alone before counting the cash. As he was counting, he noted the worn appearance and soft silky feel of the bills. ATMs always dispense crisp new bills to ensure the machine works properly. The bills in his hands were silky smooth and he looked closer. The bills were all Silver Certificates, back when the money the government printed was backed up by something other than promises. Sam looked around again at the desolate streets, knowing that $845 was worth a lot more in 1901 than a half-day's wages for a plumber. He pocketed the cash and checked all his pockets again --- no driver's license, no credit cards, just the antique cash, which was the same amount he had been carrying when he went through the rusty door. The cash and pocket watch were all he had on him. *Since I can't seem to wake from this dream, I may as well get some rest.*

Sam crossed twentieth and stood at the doors of the opulent hotel and peered inside. The lighting was dim, but he could see a clerk doing paperwork behind the ornate front desk. He was still apprehensive and walked around the corner to check out the train station across Morris. As he stood beside the hotel staring across the street at the station, he could not believe what his eyes were seeing. *This cannot be real.* The station was also quiet this time of night, although he could see a few employees stirring about inside. He stood there trying to remember what was there in 2022. The Bank For Savings building, now called Two North Twentieth, stood where the train station was. Built in 1962, the 17-story modern building was one of his favorites in the city. He didn't share Joan's affinity for architecture but fondly remembered the massive mid-century modern building because of the lighted marquee sign that spanned the top of the building in his youth and could be seen from all over the city. As he starred across the desolate street, the two-story, red brick train station looked so small in its place.

He turned to head back to the hotel and tried again to remember what had stood where this grand building was now. He was then struck by the view ahead of him. The intersection of 1st Avenue North and 20th Street, commonly referred to as the "Heaviest Corner on Earth" because of the towering skyscrapers on each corner. That was the name a national magazine had given the corner way back when the buildings were new. Sam tried to remember the story that Joan told as she led the historical tour but couldn't really come up with many details. In recent years the towers had all been renovated and large medallions placed in the concrete sidewalks at each corner proclaiming the historic title of 'World's Heaviest

Corner.' Sam walked to the corner and looked up but saw nothing but the night sky. The skyscrapers that gave the intersection the ominous title, weren't even really skyscrapers compared to modern architecture. He couldn't remember how tall the buildings were but certainly small compared to towers in other large cities and even the ones built in the 1970's and 80's just north of here, but in the early nineteen hundreds, they were definitely skyscrapers, but none of the buildings were there now.

On the northeast corner stood the ornate three-story National Bank of Birmingham where the towering Brown-Marx Building would later stand. In 2022 it was being renovated after fifty years of neglect and decay. Sam had been avoiding the construction area on his walks for months. He surveyed each corner remembering what it looked like just yesterday on his walk through the intersection.

A very plain brick building stood across the street where the Empire Building stood on his walk yesterday. Now he was looking across 1st Avenue at the Bank Restaurant and Saloon. It was a stark contrast to the most ornate building in the city built in 1909. He only remembered the date because it was in the medallion on that corner, and he stood there yesterday morning waiting on the light to change.

Across 20th Street where the John Hand Building would eventually be built was a simple but beautiful three-story brick building housing the Alabama National Bank. Sam knew that in less than ten years' time, the building along with several adjacent structures would be razed to make way for the American Trust and Savings

23

Building that would later be renamed the John Hand, after the bank's President. He had several friends that lived in the historic tower.

He turned back toward the hotel and looked at the vacant lot on the corner next to the hotel where in a short time the Woodward Building would rise. A pile of burned timbers was all that remained from the explosion and fire that took out this building and the hotel that James had described. He remembered Joan mentioning that in her tour talks but had never really thought about until now. The charred remains were pushed to the edge of the sidewalk along 1st Avenue. He noticed some crude survey stakes marking the corners of what would soon become the new tower and the first building on the heaviest corner.

The adrenaline that had kept him going was now waning and Sam felt the exhaustion of his aching body as he made his way back to the entrance of the opulent Metropolitan Hotel.

"Good evening, sir, how may I be of assistance?" The clerk greeted him as he approached the desk.

"I will need a room if you have one available," Sam responded as he eyed the spacious lobby. In the far corner, he could see a barbershop, a tailor's shop, and a large restaurant that appeared as though it would fit well into Birmingham's food scene of the 21st Century.

"Certainly. I have a very nice room on the third floor, very quiet. How long will you be staying?"

"I am not sure yet," Sam answered hoping that a good night's rest and he would awaken back in his loft and could tell this tale tonight at dinner.

"Just sign here," the clerk instructed turning a large bound book around, "I will get your key. I will keep the room for you until you decide to check out."

"Thanks," Sam said as he signed the register.

"The room rate is fifty cents per night, but we are the finest hotel in town. And that includes your breakfast. You will not find a better meal in the city," the clerk added with the stern assurance of a gifted salesman.

Sam reached in his pocket and pulled a single twenty from the fold before leaving his pocket and handed it to the clerk who now was staring at his chest.

"Oh, you are the new Marshal!" he said, "I did not realize. Chief Austin was in looking for you earlier. He was told you would be on the afternoon train from Nashville."

Sam was shocked at his words and then noticed the focus of his eyes were on the metal star pinned on the lapel of his vest that he had somehow not noticed. **U.S. Marshal** was engraved in the circle around the five-point star. It was not much different from the one he had worn in the 21st Century. Sam regained his composure and hoped his face didn't express the shock of seeing the badge pinned on his chest.

"Forgive me, but who is Chief Austin?" Sam asked hoping to not disclose his total lack of knowing what was going on.

"Conrad Austin, the Chief of Police. He is expecting you."

Sam was not sure just how to respond, but offered, "I am sure I will see him tomorrow," and took the key and headed up the stairs. His mind was now reeling again. *Did the chief have an arrest warrant for impersonating a U.S. Marshal? How was he expecting me?*

Sam made the climb to the third floor up the wide ornate staircase and found room 303. The room was spacious with a full-size bed, a nightstand, and a chest of drawers on the opposite wall. A pair of large, upholstered chairs sat in front of the window overlooking 20th Street with a view down Morris. His mind was racing with events of the last couple of hours, but the exhaustion was taking its toll. He sat on the edge of the bed and removed his boots. Before he could undress, he fell into a deep sleep.

Chapter 3

Sam awakened to the sound of train whistles blaring somewhere near and lay still, staring at the ornate tin ceiling above him. A small slice of sunlight lined across his bed from the gap in the curtains on his window. He was not in his loft. He lay there replaying the bizarre events from last night and raised his head to look down at himself. He wore white socks and the black trousers, white shirt and black vest with the star pinned to the left lapel. He sat up on the edge of the bed and saw the worn leather boots on the floor and his black jacket tossed on the back of the winged back chair in front of the window.

He stared at the dull metal star on his chest. U.S. Marshal. *What the hell is this?* The badge was not as shiny or ornate as the one he had worn for more than twelve years but it was very similar otherwise. He stood and looked around the room for the bathroom. The only door was the one he had entered through last night. He checked the watch in his pocket, 6:45. He sat back on the bed and pulled on the boots. They were surprisingly comfortable. The leather very soft and pliable. He opened the door and peered down the hallway to a door at the end with Gentlemen scrolled in a beautiful font of gold leaf paint.

After relieving what seemed like 120 years of accumulating urine, he walked to the small porcelain sink and splashed water on his face. The cold water felt good. When he opened his eyes, he couldn't believe what he was seeing in his reflection. His mostly white hair was now dark brown and about five inches longer than his normal haircut. His skin was tanned and much younger than his 58 years. He looked to be no more than 35. He remembered that tanned face from his days of playing tennis almost every day after work. He stood there, staring, and looked down at his hands. The brown splotches that had begun to dot the backs of his hands a few years ago were now gone. He splashed his face again. *At least I'm younger and in better shape in this nightmare, or whatever it is. So far, that is the only positive.*

He went back to his room and put on his jacket. He looked at himself again in the mirror and marveled at how the clothes fit his lanky body. At 6'5" buying clothes that fit had never been easy, but these fit perfectly. He looked at the image in the mirror and saw himself about thirty years and forty pounds ago. He stared at the star on his chest and was compelled to check his pockets again. *I didn't notice the star, maybe I missed something else.* He checked, but only found the watch in his vest pocket and the folded cash in his right front trouser pocket. He counted the bills again. Seven hundred and eighty dollars in twenties, four tens and a five. All well-worn and current currency of the day. He sat in the large wing chair and looked out the window across 20th street and down Morris.

The city was coming to life. Men were walking down Morris. Horses and mules pulled small wagons and he could hear the sounds of trains clanging along the tracks. *What's the plan?* After pondering his situation for several minutes, he decided his best option was to go with the flow. He had been told last night that he was expected. *How?* None of this made sense. If he decided to tell his story, he would likely be locked away in a mental hospital, so playing along was definitely the best option. He would need to get some clothes and a shave after breakfast and then look for this police chief to see if he could fill in some of the many blanks.

He headed downstairs and could smell the restaurant from the second floor as he descended the stairs. He was suddenly ravenous with hunger. Everything else could wait, he needed food. As he walked from the stairs toward his awaiting feast. The clerk from last night intercepted his path carrying a small leather duffle.

"Marshal Robbins, Good Morning," he said, "I trust you rested well and everything with your room was in order?"

"Yes. I slept well. Thank you."

"I am glad to hear. Clarence from the station brought this over for you and asked that I extend his sincere apologies for having misplaced it on your journey. They discovered it early this morning and he brought it over for you," he explained holding the bag out.

Sam reached out to grasp the bag and tried not to show more confusion.

"Would you like for me to have it taken to your room or do you need it?"

"No, you can just leave it in my room. I will check it after my breakfast," Sam said trying to stick to his plan and roll with the flow.

"Chief Austin is usually in for breakfast around 7:30 so I am sure he will find you. Is there anything else I may assist with, sir?"

"No, thank you for all your help." Sam wondered if a tip was expected, but then what would a tip be? When he stayed in hotels in

Chicago or New York, every employee encountered had their hand out and five to ten dollars was the normal, but his room was fifty cents including meals, so what would be appropriate? His thought was interrupted by the clerk's voice, snapping him back to the moment.

"Paul will take care of your breakfast. Just tell him I said to treat you well," he smiled as he turned and headed back to the desk.

As he approached the entrance of the Metropolitan Cafe, Sam was greeted by a young lady with a beaming smile who appeared to be her early twenties.

"Good morning, Marshal, it is so good to see you. Just follow me," she said nodding as she strode through the crowded tables filled with businessmen, all nattily attired. Sam followed the young hostess to a corner table in front of a window looking out on 20th street with a view down Morris.

"Thank you," he said taking a seat with his back to the corner.

"Louis will be right over to take your order," she said before heading back to her station.

Soon Louis came to take his order and within minutes Sam was presented with a mass of eggs, grits, bacon, and biscuits served on fine china plates. As he was finishing his breakfast, a distinguished gentlemen in full police uniform complete with double breasted brass button jacket approached and introduced himself.

"Good morning, Marshal Robbins, I am Police Chief Conrad Austin. It is a pleasure to finally make your acquaintance."

Sam stood and shook his hand. "Please join me," he offered motioning to the empty chair across the table.

Austin stood about 5'9" with a slight build that looked beefier with the uniform. He had a drooping mustache that covered his top lip and curved upward precariously at each end. He carried his cap in hand and took a seat and ordered coffee.

"I expected your arrival on the afternoon train yesterday, but could not locate you," he said rather sternly.

Sam, rolling with the flow, made the decision to stay as close to the truth as he could.

"Yes, I apologize for that. I am not sure what exactly happened still. I may have been ill or hit my head somehow, but I have no recollection of my arrival. My first memory is late last night about two blocks from here. It was quite odd, to say the least, so I apologize if you were inconvenienced."

"No worries, but perhaps you may want to see the doctor? I can recommend one."

"I seem to be fine this morning but thank you."

"As you are likely aware, Mr. Lesser, Mayor Drennen, Sheriff O'Brien and a great many others worked very hard to get you here. But you may not be aware that they all have different reasons for doing so."

Sam's head was spinning again with this information as he consciously tried to not look overwhelmed by the report that he was supposed to know. *Mayor and Sheriff were obvious but who was Mr. Lesser and others?* He was anxious to hear just what brought him here, so he continued to roll with the flow. He leaned into the table and looked in Austin's brown eyes.

"How so?"

"Well, firstly, they are all politicians at heart. And, even though I too am an elected official, I have served as a Police Officer much of my adult life as did my father, one of the first officers in this city," he began and continued to layout his thoughts on the matter. "I do think they all have the best intentions to improve the city, but none have experience in law enforcement. The city is growing rapidly with all the commerce and building underway, and our police force is very understaffed. Many see this as an opportunity to turn this into a city like New York or Chicago, but it is now a rough and rowdy town filled with miners, immigrants, and ruffians. Those that profit from saloons and gambling are not so anxious for change, while others may be too anxious. Neither see an increased police force as a necessary means and so here we are. Normally, the U.S. Marshal is also a politician, but my understanding is that you are a lawman like myself, so I am ready to work with you and hear your plans."

Sam's brain was in overdrive digesting the information. He tread carefully to get more information without exposing just how clueless he really was.

"I am anxious to learn more before I commit to any plans, so I look forward to hearing more and learning more about Birmingham. I am certainly not a politician, so you have no worries there. Do I have an office or a place to work?"

"Yes, your predecessor mainly worked from his home and spent a good deal of time traveling the district, but with his passing and your appointment, you may choose to work differently. I understand that you have assigned deputies to cover most of the northern regions and you plan to work here. Is this correct?"

Sam again was learning more about himself than anything else and knew that the Northern District of Alabama was the same as it was in 2022, covering the northern half of the state from just south of Birmingham.

"Yes, I plan to spend most of my time here in the city, but I can assure you that I will not interfere in your operations. I am here to assist," Sam assured him, assuming that the longstanding friction between local and federal law enforcement agencies went back to this era as well.

"I am glad to hear that," Austin smiled with a slight hint of relief. "We can certainly use any assistance from the government and a man of your reputation. Your office is in the new city hall. Would you like me to walk you over there?"

"No, I have a few things to finish up, but I will make my way there later this morning."

"Fine, then. When you arrive, come to my office and I will make the introductions there," he said as he stood and reached out to shake hands again.

Sam stood and shook his hand.

"I assume you've already met Mr. Lesser and Paul, here?" Austin asked.

"No. No, I haven't."

"Well, let us remedy that," Austin said looking around the restaurant. He spotted a tall thin man on the other side of the restaurant. His sleeves were rolled up and his necktie was tucked into his shirt and a towel was tossed over his shoulder. Austin motioned to him, and he headed over.

"Paul, this is the new U.S. Marshal, Sam Robbins," Austin started the introductions. "Paul is not only a partner and restaurant owner here in the hotel, but he also owns and operates Paul's Café over on 19th Street and leads the 2nd Regiment of Alabama Troops Militia and now is a landowner with orchards and farms just out of the city."

The two men shook hands.

"Paul Gilardoni, sir. It is a pleasure to meet you, Marshall," he said with a distinctive Italian accent. "Do not be put off by that description. I am but a man striving to make a living for his family, and I do so by providing food," he smiled. "I recently purchased some land and have planted trees and vines, but it will likely be my children that will enjoy those fruits."

"It is a pleasure to meet you, sir," Sam offered. "My stay here and my meal were excellent."

"Have you met Emil, yet? I think he is here today."

"No, I have not," Sam answered.

"Emil Lesser is the hotel owner and he has several business ventures in the city," Austin added.

"Come! We meet him now," Paul said leading the men toward the rear of the hotel lobby to a large office.

Emil Lesser was a distinguished looking man in his late forties. Dressed in a fine suit, his mustache rivaled Conrad Austin's in both fullness and curled edges. It covered his mouth completely. He spoke with a heavy accent that seemed to be both Russian and German, but his

English was perfect. The men exchanged pleasantries and promises of meeting again soon before parting ways.

Sam headed up to his room and anxiously located the leather bag sitting on the floor at the foot his bed. He sat in the chair and opened the bag. Two shirts like the one he was wearing. A pair of trousers very similar to the ones he wore, only with a faint gray stripe. Underwear and socks. He lay the garments aside and reached for a small leather pouch inside the bag. He opened it to find a shaving brush, small ceramic bowl, and straight razor. He instinctively felt the stubble on his face. *That ain't gonna happen. I would cut my own throat.* He reached in for another leather bag and pulled it out. It was much heavier. The leather was not a bag but a simple piece of leather that wrapped the Colt revolver he now held. It was a crude firearm compared to the guns he had carried during his career, and even the Smith and Wesson revolver his father had taught him to shoot as a young teenager, but it was beautiful and no doubt an effective weapon in 1901. He reached in and pulled out the last remaining item, a black leather gun belt and holster. He gasped aloud when he saw the stamped lettering on the underside of the wide belt --- *Sam Robbins.*

Chapter 4

Sam put on a fresh shirt and stared at the pistol and gun belt lying on the chair. He strapped on the gun belt and emptied the six bullets from the Colt. It was clean and looked to be well used but in fine working order. He could tell it had been meticulously cared for. He didn't know much about revolvers, especially antique ones. He knew that the guns in the old western movies he watched as a kid with his dad were all single action and seemed to have endless amounts of bullets as you rarely saw a cowboy have to reload. He checked the cylinder again to ensure it was safe and dry-fired the weapon and was pleased to discover it was at least double action. He counted the shells inserted neatly in the leather loops on his left side of his belt – twelve. Two reloads.

He remembered as a child watching his dad load his revolver every day before heading to work. He purposely did it without looking. He told him that if he ever was in a situation that he needed to reload, he had to keep his eyes on his surroundings. It was something they taught in the academy, but he had also learned most of that in his two tours in Viet Nam.

By the time Sam was in the academy, semi-auto pistols were the only things being used. The few old-timers who still carried revolvers used speed loader devices that could drop in six rounds in the cylinder with a simple twist. If you insisted on carrying a wheel-gun, as they were loving referred to, speed loaders were mandatory and before Sam made Sergeant revolvers had become extinct on the force.

Sam stood in front of the smoky mirror in his room loading and unloading the weapon. He was surprised at how efficient he became after a few times. It was as though his memories of watching his father do it rubbed off on him although he had never done it himself.

He stood looking at the younger version of his reflection in the mirror with the gun strapped to his hip under his jacket. He had carried a firearm most of his adult life and the silhouette in the foggy mirror looked familiar and bizarre at the same time. He looked like he had stepped out of a movie from his childhood, but the gun felt comfortable. He looked at the star pinned on his chest and still couldn't imagine how this was happening. *It can't be real.*

He dropped his key at the front desk on his way out. A different clerk was now on duty but still greeted him by name. Sam knew to drop the key off at the desk from his stays in small hotels in Paris when he and Joan were able to vacation there. It was as if the French were immune from modern technology where hotel keys became cheap plastic cards with magnetic strips or worse yet a phone app. Paris was one of their favorite places to visit and they had looked forward to more extended stays once they retired but that was not meant to be. Sam thought about Joan and what she would make of this crazy dream or whatever it was. As a history teacher, she would love this and would not be flying as blind as he felt.

As Sam stepped out of the hotel, he was amazed at the bustle of the busy city around him. As a child, before white flight completely emptied the city of retail, he remembered Saturdays shopping with his mom and the streets being busy, but not this busy. There were people everywhere. He made his way to the corner of 1st Avenue North and stood again and marveled at what he knew would become the "Heaviest Corner on Earth" within the decade. Now, the tallest building was four-stories. Many of the buildings were simple wooden structures that would have easily been at home in a western movie set. The city looked so different in the light of day. It was busy but so very different with all the horses and wagons. The few women he saw were all dressed in heavy dresses to the ground with long sleeves. Almost all the men had moustaches or beards. Everyone wore a hat.

As he made his way up 20th, he continued to be struck by the sparseness although all the lots were filled, there were no high rises. Most were simple one or two-story commercial buildings. But there were also grand Victorian homes and simple frame houses strewn in too.

When he reached 4th Avenue, he looked west to see the gleaming, brand new City Hall on the southeast corner of 4th and 19th. The red brick building stood four-stories tall and had a massive tower that extended the height another two stories. Sam had been able to see the tower from the corner of 1st and 20th and used it to navigate the city that was so familiar and yet so unrecognizable to him.

He found Austin inside and spent the rest of the morning touring the new city hall, meeting city leaders and police officers as well as an assortment of other men. The only person that Sam met that he was familiar with was a city alderman named George Ward. Sam was most familiar with the name although he couldn't remember ever seeing a photograph of the man with the storied reputation. He was a bit struck to meet the man that was so young and engaging. Joan had researched this man and lectured often about him and his progressive politics. Sam remembered reading about his expansive estate that sprawled along the crest in what was now the suburban city of Vestavia Hills, named after the sprawling estate Ward had named Vestavia.

Sam had played softball and tennis often at George Ward Park on the city's south side. It was surreal to meet a man that history had recorded and kept his name familiar for more a century. Ward was very cordial and had evidently also played a vital role in bringing Sam to Birmingham.

His last introduction was to Mayor Walter Melville "Mel" Drennen, one of the last men to emerge from the just concluded Aldermen meeting. He too was cordial and made a point that Sam knew he was instrumental in bringing the new Marshall to the city and had high expectations.

Sam was surprised to see the total absence of any women, not only in the meeting aftermath, but also in general. The city hall seemed to be an all-male domain.

Throughout the morning, Sam was continually surprised that each man he met seemed to know much more about him than he certainly did. It was as though he was a rock star marshal. What would this be like with Twitter and Facebook to further this reputation, he thought once as young police officer told him about all the things he had read about him and actually seemed to gush at the chance to meet his hero.

Through his rounds of the morning Sam had pieced together a bit of history on Sam Robbins, the U.S. Marshal of 1901.

He hailed from somewhere around Louisville, Kentucky and gained quite a reputation for single handedly bringing down a gang of outlaws that had terrorized Kentucky and Tennessee for more than a decade. As a young Deputy Marshal, it seems that Sam confronted the bandits during a bank robbery in Bardstown and killed three of them, wounded two more and arrested another despite having taken a bullet in his own right leg.

Later he served as Deputy Marshal in eastern Tennessee and one week ago was appointed Marshal to the Northern Alabama District after a group of local businessmen and city leaders, Congressmen, and State Senators petitioned the new President, Theodore Roosevelt, into helping with the growing crime in the new city of Birmingham.

In only his second week in office following the assassination of President McKinley, Teddy Roosevelt had tapped Sam Robbins to be the new U.S. Marshal of the Northern District of Alabama.

Finally, Chief Austin showed Sam to his office. The small office on the third floor was unremarkable but Sam was surprised to see his name in gold leaf paint on the milky glass pane of the door. Inside were a small desk and four chairs, a filing cabinet and small bookcase. A door behind the desk led to Sam's office.

"You will need to hire a new clerk," Austin advised pointing to the front desk. "Ballard left and went back to Selma after Hill died. He was not very efficient anyway," he added.

Sam walked into the larger office with a larger desk and more bookshelves filled with what appeared to be law books. A crude rolling chair made of solid oak sat behind the desk. A coat rack stood solemnly in the corner. Sam looked out of the window onto 4th Avenue below.

"Hill never saw this place, so none of his personal belongings are here. We all just moved into the new building a few months ago. He was working from home when it happened, but I think he had an office up in Huntsville."

Sam had also pieced together that his predecessor had met his untimely death about two months earlier somewhere around the resort town of Blount Springs, north of Birmingham. The details were still sketchy, and Sam didn't want to blow it by asking questions that he should already know the answers to.

"I will leave you to it, Marshall," Austin said reaching for the door. "I will give you a few days to get settled but please call on me if you need anything."

"Thanks so much, Chief," Sam said extending his hand to the mustached man who seemed small and frail without his uniform jacket. "I will be in touch soon and we can talk. I am sure I will have a list of questions and I really do appreciate your help."

Sam sat in the wooden chair behind the desk and was surprised to find it was not uncomfortable as he imagined. It looked so crude compared to the modern desk chairs with fancy formed padded seats and reclining backs. The oak seemed to have just the right curve for his butt and a heavy spring mechanism allowed the back to recline about three inches, which was just enough.

Sam started by going through the mound of mail on his desk and started with a large envelope stuffed with handwritten reports. Among them was the death report made by the Sherriff of Blount County on his predecessor, U.S. Marshal Otis Lawrence Hill. Other than the overly ornate penmanship and formal English wording, the report was straight forward but short on any detail. The Marshal was found dead near of one of the many springs surrounding the Hotel and Spa Resort there. The death was assumed a natural one although the Marshal was only 51 years old and there was no explanation in the report to justify that assumption. In an accompanying report from U.S. Deputy Marshall, Angus McClure, he wrote that when he arrived from Huntsville two days after the body was discovered. He spoke with a doctor who was vacationing at the resort who had examined the body and stated that he had surmised that the Marshal had fallen and struck his forehead on a nearby rock outcropping and died before a maid at the hotel discovered his body. It could not be determined whether the Marshal had a health event that caused him to fall or the fall itself killed him. The Marshal had stopped at the resort on his way to Birmingham from Huntsville as he often did. No witnesses to the actual event could be found.

Reading the reports, Sam realized that he was getting more used to the proper language used in the day. It seemed that no one used contractions, and everyone spoke the Queen's English except for the few immigrants he had encountered. Although both Paul and Emil had heavy accents, their English was perfect. Sam wondered where the language had begun to degrade and what would the texting and Twitter shorthand do to further that decay. He put the reports aside and continued opening mail.

After more than an hour he had amassed several stacks as he continued to sort through the mound of envelopes. He had encountered court orders on a number of cases to be filed. He had opened two warrants and a summons to be served. He had read two complaints penned by concerned citizens about the lack of enforcement of liquor and gambling laws in the City of Birmingham.

At least there is no junk mail, Sam thought as he gave his eyes a break and leaned back in the chair. He pulled out his watch from his vest pocket – 11:28. He looked at the piles of papers neatly arranged in stacks on the desk and the still unopened pile of envelopes which was now manageable. *I can knock this out*, he thought reaching for the next envelope.

He immediately felt the heft and texture of the paper in his hand. It felt like a proper wedding invitation that one would receive before things were done through zoom chats and emails. Most of the mail he had opened was addressed simply to the Marshal in one or more various forms, but this one was different. *To the Honorable Samuel Robbins, United States Marshal*, scrolled in what he would consider fine calligraphy. He flipped over the envelope to see a startling return address – *The Office of the President of the United States of America / President Theodore Roosevelt, Jr.* Sam carefully opened the envelope expecting to find some official appointment letter from a bureaucrat in the White House. Sam knew that the Marshal Service, although the oldest law enforcement agency in the U.S. was not a federalized service until 1957. Prior to that, each Marshal was appointed by the President and served at his pleasure. There was no central organization at the Federal level until 1957.

Sam was astounded when he removed the heavy paper from the envelope to find a handwritten letter from the President. Over the three pages, Roosevelt first wrote of Sam's worthiness of his new position and the importance that he felt this new industrial city held in this new century to modernize the country and finally heal the wounds of the Civil War. He commended Sam on his service and reminded him that he too had served as the President of the Commission of Police in New York City just seven years earlier. He wrote that in that position his eyes were opened to the travesties that exist when the law and other government resources are not applied uniformly. He wrote that he witnessed the chasm between those who have much and those struggling to survive. He also found the importance in making those who govern and enforce the laws abide by those same laws. Sam then was gripped by the president's closing paragraph:

In closing, I want to assure you that you have the full support of not only myself, but that of the entire U.S. Government. Birmingham is at a critical junction of growth not only as a fine city, but also as an integral part of this nation. I have heard many concerns from legislators, city leaders, and citizens about a number of concerns from lawless operations to corruption within the government. I have the utmost faith in your leadership to sort out the truth and uphold the law and to right the direction of this fine city and region. Thank you again for your service.

    Sam leaned back in the chair and stared at the letter in his hand. *How many handwritten letters have the last several Presidents written,* he thought. He opened the last three envelopes and added their contents to the appropriate stacks on the desk. He placed the President's letter in the top drawer of his desk. It was otherwise empty, so he checked the others. The bottom drawer on the right contained the personnel files of two deputies assigned to various parts of the district. The other drawers were all empty. He looked at his watch – 12:41, time for lunch.

    As Sam stepped out of City Hall onto the sidewalk of 4th Avenue North, he stood and surveyed the city. *What do I know about policing in this era? There are no resources that I am familiar with.* He decided he would get some lunch and find some new clothes and look for a place to clean the ones he had. *A shower would feel great. Do they have showers or am I going to be bathing in a creek or something?* He turned onto 19th street and headed back to the hotel.

Chapter 5

Sam ate lunch at Paul's Café on 19th street and again saw the owner, Paul Gilardoni, who came in while he was dining. Paul said that he liked to check in to both his restaurants at mealtimes to make sure everything was "first class." He told Sam that he was also the proprietor of the Black Cat Saloon on 2nd Avenue North, offering liquor, wine, and fine cigars. Paul also told him that there were two tailor shops in the Metropolitan Hotel – People's Tailoring on the ground floor and F. Smith Tailor located on the 2nd Floor. He preferred Frank Smith "as he did all the work himself and had a fine attention to detail and worked quickly and at a reasonable charge."

Paul also informed the new Marshal that the Metropolitan Hotel had a very nice bathroom for gentlemen with hot and cold running water, although if he preferred having a woman assist, he could recommend Lou Wooster's place on 4th Avenue. Sam thanked him and hoped that his face didn't show the recognition of the famed Madame's mention. Joan had also lectured about the infamous Birmingham Madame who claimed to have an affair with John Wilkes Booth and was praised and fondly remembered for her service along with her ladies for nursing the young city through a cholera epidemic in 1873. UAB gave an annual award in her name for exemplary service in public health.

After a hot bath at the hotel, Sam went to visit Mr. Frank Smith and was measured for two suits, one black and one gray, and two extra trousers for each. He ordered three white shirts and two vests, which he learned were actually called waistcoats, since he had grown to like the one he was wearing. His total bill was $17.50, and Frank promised the Marshal he would have one suit ready in two days' time and would get the second one finished within the week.

Sam spent the rest of the afternoon in his room reading the three newspapers he picked up in the lobby. The more he could learn about current events, the better he could figure out how to handle himself. He also stopped in the public library located in a small building adjacent to the new City Hall before leaving, hoping to find a book on time travel or some magic formula that might explain his current predicament, but that was a bust.

After perusing the newspapers for most of the afternoon, Sam could think of nothing but his situation. If this was a dream or the result of a head injury, he needed to figure out how to wake up. He had read once that dreams, even ones that seemed like full-length movies, really only lasted a few seconds because your brain could process subconscious thoughts so much faster. *Can I force myself to wake up? What if I'm not asleep and this is real?*

Sam was an avid reader of fiction but was not really a fan of sci-fi or fantasy. He found them too unbelievable to draw him into the story, but that may change with this experience. As he sat staring out the window at the busy city of 1901, he considered the only book about time travel he had read was the novel by Stephen King, *11/22/63*. Sam had read the book probably 10 years ago when it was new because Joan was fascinated by the historical context in it. As an historian, she punched a few holes in some of the minor details but loved the premise. Sam found the movie version a couple of years ago on TV late one night when he was desperate for some entertainment. He ended up staying up all night to finish the series in one sitting.

The story begins with an all but defunct diner in a small town and the owner of the diner steps through a secret portal in a back door of the pantry and is transported from 2011 back to 1958. When the owner discovers he is dying from a terminal illness, he recruits a regular customer, a local schoolteacher, to take over his quests back in time. His mission has been to figure out a way to stop President Kennedy, who at the time hasn't yet been elected, from being assassinated. In the novel the premise is set early on, and the schoolteacher is given two rules about the time travel. Once you go, no matter how long you stay – an hour or years, when you return, only two minutes have passed. Each time you go back, there is a full reset, and everything starts to unfold again as it did in 1958.

As far as Sam could recall King didn't delve into particulars of the actual voyage of time travel. No mention of money differences or technologies. He simply has the dying man convincing the schoolteacher to take up the cause. "Save Kennedy, save his brother. Save Martin Luther King. Stop the race riots. Stop Vietnam, maybe.... Get rid of one wretched waif, buddy, and you could save millions of lives."

It turns out the man had made numerous trips back and had never been able to foil the assassination but learned something with each venture. Eventually the teacher is successful but then discovers his success was not at all what he envisioned.

Until this moment, Sam hadn't even thought about consequences of altering past events. He hadn't thought about the big picture at all other than being appalled at the treatment of women and people of color in his one day in this era. He had grown up in Birmingham and was certainly aware of the struggle for civil rights. He was born on the same day as the 16th Street Baptist Church was bombed by the Ku Klux Klan, killing four young girls and injuring others. As a white kid in the south, he knew about the injustices that he saw and was aware of his privilege being white, even after laws had long been established to remove inequality based on race. His father was a rookie cop in the city and dealt with changes that would come ever so slowly. Even when Sam joined the force in 1985, prejudice was rampant in the department and in society, but nothing compared to what he had witnessed in the past twenty-four hours.

As he looked out his window down Morris, he thought about the young man who found him sitting in the street and was reluctant to shake his hand until making sure no one was watching. He now understood the fear of that simple action. Slavery was technically over, but it wasn't really. He had learned that blacks who weren't gainfully employed were arrested for vagrancy or any number of other charges and sentenced to maximum jail terms and then leased out to the local coal or ore mines and fabrication plants as prisoner labor. Still slaves. No longer picking cotton but instead working far more dangerous jobs so white men could get richer. In many ways, the system was far worse than slavery. The new masters had no real investment in the workers. If they dropped dead, the "masters" would just call the state for replacements. It was a reprehensible system of injustice. *What can I do to stop that from escalating further?* Sam then thought of the outcome of the world that the protagonist in King's novel came home to after he thought he had changed the world for good. It was not the intended outcome by a long shot. *I just need to figure out how to get home.*

After dinner at the hotel, Sam strolled through downtown. He discovered that once the sun went down the only activity seemed to be around the many saloons along the streets. Not all that different from 2022 he thought. In the loft district there were dozens of bars within three blocks of his loft and twice as many restaurants. But as he strolled down 1st Avenue, he noticed that most of the restaurants were closing, and it was only seven o'clock. The saloons on the other hand were cranking up.

Sam walked to 24th Street and looked at where his loft building would be in 2022. The old five story warehouse that was his home was built in 1923 so a brick two-story building was there. It appeared to be a wholesale grocery supply business. It was difficult to comprehend that his century old building was not yet built.

From the corner he looked south where the viaduct would later span the railroad reservation, Morris, and Powell Avenues. Instead, he saw the sidewalk slowly descending to Morris, no viaduct. In between the buildings lining Morris, he could see the tracks behind as a freight train passed. The dirt street crossed the tracks to his left in the distance. Another train chugged by going the opposite direction.

He turned and walked down Morris. As he walked, he saw men loading and unloading wagons into buildings along the tracks. Just like the first night, it all looked so familiar and so foreign at the same time. He had yet to see an automobile. As he approached 21st Street he saw the flickering glow emanating from the blacksmith shop ahead.

Sam stopped and looked around and then walked to the middle of the cobblestone street and stood. *This was where I was.* He slowly turned making a full three-hundred-and-sixty-degree rotation. No rusty doors. No blinding lights. *If the door was the passage back home, then how?* If King had it right and the door was some sort of portal, the viaduct would not be built for another seventeen years. *Am I stuck here until then?*

In King's book, when the protagonist lands in 1958, there is no diner... he just lands in the lot amongst the passersby who never seemed to notice that a man just appeared out of nowhere. *How did he go back?* Sam racked his brain but couldn't remember the sequence for re-entry to the 21st century. *Why am I obsessing over this? It is fiction! I don't know what this is, but I have got to get out of this.*

As Sam headed back to the hotel, he noticed that James was standing watching him from the doorway of the shop but ducked back inside when their eyes met. As he approached the shop, he peeked inside but James was nowhere to be seen.

As Sam climbed the hotel stairs, he hoped that when he woke up tomorrow, he would find himself at home in his loft and this nightmare would be over.

Chapter 6

Sam did not wake up in his loft but found himself once again in the 1901 hotel room. If this was a dream or the result of some head injury, surely it would end soon. Whatever it was, it seemed all too real. Sam was still dealing with the fact that he had been expected and many of the people he had met knew more about him than he certainly did. *Could my memories of 2022 and that time, be the delusion?* He considered the possibility, and it made no more sense than anything else of the last few days, so he started another day in his new reality and spent the next several days establishing a new routine.

Surprisingly the paperwork required by the U.S. Marshal was not all that different from the next century, just much less volume. In 2022 it had increased by thousands of times, but by then most of it was handled electronically and by a staff of dozens of people. Not having a central D.C. office seemed to streamline most processes causing Sam to lament the bureaucracy that the country would be burdened with in the next century.

In one of the stacks of mail Sam had opened on that first day were five applications for the open clerk position. Over the next two days, Sam interviewed three candidates in person and hired Charles Weston, a young lad from Montgomery who worked in the U.S. Marshal Office of the Middle District of Alabama that covered roughly the eastern half of Southern Alabama. Sam learned that the office had a total of three clerks and Charles was the junior of the three and was looking to make a move. The young man of twenty was well spoken and well educated and looked forward to establishing roots in the young city of Birmingham.

Sam figured he wouldn't have to teach him the processes and the young man could likely teach him things. In the 21st Century, Sam only had a basic understanding of the paperwork in the office, so Charles's experience would be most helpful.

With the burden of mundane office operations off his plate, Sam took the opportunity to get familiar with the city as it was now. He took daily walks and met the movers and shakers who were anxious to make his acquaintance, but he also made a point to meet the people – shop owners, bartenders, and workers. The city was so different than he could have ever imagined yet in many ways it was also familiar.

Sam still had trouble getting use to the way African Americans were so blatantly mistreated and the lack of women in the workforce, although as he moved around he found more and more women working against all odds. There were the expected saloon girls, but he also found women running successful businesses. Some had inherited the business from a father or husband, but a few were self-starters who would make any modern woman proud. They couldn't vote and had no real standing in society, yet here they were forging through life.

The most remarkable example Sam had discovered was Dr. Irene Bullard, a medical doctor who had a small practice in the Watts Building at the corner of 20th Street and 3rd Avenue North. The building was a nice four-story brick structure but would be dwarfed by the Watts Tower that Sam remembered from 2022. It was definitely an historic building, but obviously like Sam's loft building, it would built sometime later.

Dr. Bullard was a shy but confident woman making her way in a man's world. Sam had been introduced to her at a lunch hosted by Alderman George Ward. He was seated next to Irene and through the course of lunch got to know a little about her, discovering they both shared a passion for music and live theatre, and she promised to show him all the opportunities of entertainment in the new city.

After two weeks of nonstop work, Charles was settled and the backlog of paperwork had been processed, Sam took the morning train to Huntsville to meet with his two deputies. One, Angus McClure, was stationed in what would later become known as the Rocket City – Huntsville, and the other, Michael Isbell, in the northwest corner of the state in the town of Tuscumbia. Sam was eager to meet the deputies he had only corresponded with by telegram and letter. He found both young lads to be genuine, hard-working men who had grown up in their respective communities.

Sam had asked Angus to supply him with all his notes about his investigation of the death of Marshal Hill. He was pleased to see the young deputy had very thoroughly documented his interviews with everyone at the resort.

After a three-hour visit, Sam had to catch the train back to Birmingham, but he had one more bit of news to share. The Deputy Marshals were thrilled when Sam informed them that he was increasing their monthly salaries from $50 to $60.

Sam had learned that he received $250 each month for salaries and another $100 for supplies and expenses. He hired Charles at a $50 rate which left $80 for his own pay. With a satisfied staff, Sam thought he could spend more time on trying to figure out how to make his way back home. If this was real and he had somehow been transported back in time, then there had to be a way back.

Sam arrived back at Union Station in time to complete his daily routine that always ended with a stroll down Morris Avenue after dinner. He always stopped at the spot and studied every detail of his surroundings. He had finally remembered that in the King novel and subsequent TV series, the protagonist Jake would make his way back to the empty lot where the diner would eventually stand with its magic pantry door to the past. With no diner and no door, Jake would find the invisible step and go through the door that couldn't be seen. *I know it's a fictional story but what else do I have?*

Sam began to walk back and forth along the sidewalk carefully and methodically as he tried to imagine where the door was on the bridge supports that were not there yet. Unlike that first night, Morris was not completely desolate most nights as men milled about but their presence was scarce as most of the activities were along 1st and 2nd Avenues where saloons and brothels drew most of the traffic. Sam was aware that his actions would certainly look strange to passersby, so he tried to be discreet. Each night he expanded his grid but never felt anything, and certainly didn't stumble through a portal.

He prayed each night that in the morning he would awaken in his own bed in his loft in 2022 and this long dream, or whatever it was, would end, but each morning he awoke to a new day in his new reality.

      Sam had now been in his routine for more than month. Thanksgiving had just passed and although a designated national holiday, it was not really celebrated in the city. Sam had only heard casual mentions of it as the city began to prepare for Christmas. He remembered 21st century Thanksgivings with friends and family. It was always an intimate, small gathering with a few friends, but Joan loved to make a feast and he missed that. Mostly, he missed her.

      As Sam left Paul's Café that evening after a fine dinner, he stood on 19th and noticed the full moon in the gray sky. The night air was chilly with a slight breeze blowing. Sam was thankful for the warm coat that Frank Smith had just delivered and the wide brim fedora he picked up at Bon Ton Hatters earlier in the day. As he walked back toward Morris, the moon cast an orange glow on the storefronts, and he remembered that first night. *There was a full moon! Maybe that is the key... maybe tonight will be the night!* He quickened his pace as he turned onto Morris. The train station seemed busier than usual tonight as people came and went as he passed by, and he saw his first automobile. He wasn't sure what it was, maybe a Model-T, but a man was strapping a trunk into the back and fired up the choppy engine and pulled away as Sam reached the corner.

The street grew quieter as he approached 21st Street and he looked skyward to see the big orange moon looming above and he had a renewed hope as he began his methodical pacing starting on the sidewalk and working toward the center of the street where he woke up that night. Before each pass he looked around to make sure no one was witnessing this bizarre ritual.

As he stood in the center of the cobblestone street, he looked up again at the moon and a sense of doom flooded through his body. *There is no magic. No portal. No invisible door. I am stuck here.* As he walked back to the sidewalk, he sensed something at the corner of the building, and he froze staring at the dark space between the two buildings that was less than three feet wide.

James Lewis stepped from the shadows and onto the moonlit sidewalk and tipped his hat. Sam's heart skipped a beat, but his breath returned at the sight of James. He had only seen glimpses of the man since that first night. It seemed as though he was avoiding him every time he passed by the blacksmith shop.

"Evenin' Marshal," James said with just a hint of a smile.

"Good evening, James," Sam answered in relief as he approached the man that looked as though he could easily fend for himself in a dark alley. Despite the chill in the air, he was dressed the same, jeans and a heavy leather apron, no shirt. His black biceps and shoulders glistened with sweat in the moonlight.

"I haven't seen you much lately," he said as he extended his hand to James.

60

James, as before, paused and scanned the perimeter before meeting it with his own beefy hand in a firm handshake.

"How have you been?" Sam asked as the men stood on the sidewalk.

"Ah, I been fine," James responded as his smile grew slightly, revealing his white teeth that seemed to glimmer in the moonlight. "You gettin' settled in?"

"I am. I am learning my way around the city and meeting a lot of folks," Sam said to keep the conversation going. After a brief and somewhat awkward pause of silence he saw James's face grow serious as his head dropped for moment.

"Misser Sam, you mind if I ax you a question?" he finally said with slight quiver in his voice as if he summoned all his courage to ask if he could ask.

"Of course. You can ask me anything, James."

James slowly raised his head as his eyes met Sam's under the eerie sky and then he glanced around to make sure they were still alone on the darkened street. Then his eyes met Sam's as he again seemed to force out the words.

"I's wonerdin' if you know a man... a man named Elvis... Elvis Presley?"

The question literally took Sam's breath away. As he gasped, his mouth agape. James was staring at him awaiting his answer. *Could this be? How else would he know about Elvis forty years or more before his birth? Was the King named after someone? Did I miss that somehow?* Sam caught his breath as his mind continued to race and process the question and then considered his answer carefully.

"Does this Elvis wear blue suede shoes?" he asked looking deep into the man's eyes and he saw the sparkle before the biggest grin filled his face.

"YES! Yes, he does!" James almost shouted and again scanned the perimeter to ensure they were still alone.

The two men stood staring at one another. Sam was beaming too. "Does this mean..."

James held his fingers in front of his mouth and made a loud SHHHHH.

"Not here," he advised in an almost whisper. "Let's go back to the shop," he nodded.

Chapter 7

The men walked hurriedly to the blacksmith shop and James scanned the street again before pulling the large door closed.

"Back here," James pointed to a rough wooden door just past the horse stall in the back of the building. The small room with hay strewn on the floor appeared to be James's home. A thicker pile of hay in the corner was his bed. A small table and two mis-matched wooden chairs were the only furnishing other than the oil lantern he hung on a hook on the wall.

"We can talk safely in here," James said motioning for Sam to take the other chair. His heavy African American Southern drawl that Sam hadn't heard since his youth was now gone. Sam's mind was reeling, and he didn't know where to begin but suddenly found himself blurting out the obvious question.

"Are you from the future?" he said excitedly.

James was still smiling from ear to ear but was a bit more subdued as he had been planning this moment for weeks since the first time he saw Sam floundering in the street at the same exact place he woke up over two years ago. He had been observing Sam's nightly ritual ever since, but knew he had to be absolutely sure before approaching him.

"Yes, Sam I am. I have been here for a little over two years trying to figure out the puzzle of getting back. I had really abandoned hope until you came along. I had almost convinced myself that it was some crazy nightmare or something, but I know things that haven't happened yet, so I really couldn't convince myself, but I had all but given up hope of finding any answers until that night I saw you."

"So, you knew that first night?" Sam asked surprised again by this news.

"Not for certain," James explained, "but you ended up in the very same place I did two years ago, and I've been watching you look for answers every night in that same place."

"Wow, so you landed in that same spot... that is very interesting, although I'm disappointed to learn you have been here for two years. Where did you come from? What year was it?" Sam asked in rapid fire finally spilling the queue of questions that were forming in his mind.

"I was right here in Birmingham, in pretty much that same spot only it was 1963. I was trying to get away from some guys who were going to do me harm and I ducked into a door under an overpass that spans the street out there but, BOOM... I ended up here in boots and tee shirt and jeans with the forty-seven dollars I had in my pocket and nothing else."

"Was the door a stairwell in the viaduct?" Sam asked.

"I am not really sure, but I was hoping it was. Those guys were closing in on me and I was looking for a way out. I tried several doors on the buildings as I came down Morris and the one under the bridge opened. I was blinded by this intense light and the temp was freezing. I felt hyperthermia setting in, but I was disoriented by then and could no longer find the door. I remember things fading to black and then I woke up in the street just like you did. Except no one saw me.   I wondered around for the rest of the night and a family over on Avenue A took me in and fed me and let me stay there for a couple of days. My first clue was that they lived on Avenue A... in my time, that street is 1st Avenue South. Then I saw a calendar on their kitchen wall, and it was 1899. After a couple of weeks my money was running out, so I got a job here. I used to help my grandfather do this when I was a kid. What about you?   Are you from Birmingham?"

"Yes, I am," Sam began as his mind was digesting James's story... *two years ago... 1963... same place on Morris... same door.* "I came through probably that same door underneath the 21st Street bridge, but I was in the year 2022." Sam saw the shock on James's face at that news, but he didn't say anything, so Sam continued. "I had pretty much the same experience... the light... the cold... when I opened my eyes, I was relieved that the first thing I saw was the moon and I knew that I had gotten out, but I was so weak as you saw. I was sure this was all the result of a head injury or a dream but now it's real," Sam said as his own words weighed heavy on the reality.

"2022... for real?" James asked as his mind could not comprehend that date.

"Yep... I had retired from the U.S. Marshal Service two weeks before this and I end up here with the cash I was carrying only it's now Silver Certificates... my iPhone is now a pocket watch and I am wearing this star," he said shaking his head.

"What's an eye-phone? Is that like eyeglasses or something?"

Sam chuckled. He was so consumed with the missing 121 years that he hadn't given any thought to the fifty-nine years between them.

"It's actually a telephone. It's about the size of a pack of cigarettes and as thin as a match book..."

"And it works like a regular telephone?" James asked with amazement at the thought of such a futuristic device.

"Yes, they came into existence in the 1980's but by the turn of the century they were commonplace and had greatly evolved beyond just a phone."

"How do they work? I mean do you have to plug into a phone line?"

Sam chuckled again, "No they are wireless... I am not smart enough to explain it. The phone companies put up millions of towers all over the world and the phones send and receive signals through them, but they are also high-powered computers too."

James's face showed even more confusion. "But you said it was the size of a pack of cigarettes, right? I am familiar with computer technology but those take up entire buildings!"

"Not in 2022... In the eighties desktop computers became the norm but by the turn of the century a phone had more capacity than old main frame computers a decade earlier and by 2022, they were far more advanced, and it gets better each year. I didn't even know computers were a thing in the sixties... what did you do?"

"I had just finished Medical School," James explained. "I came home for a break before starting my internship and was helping with the protests and organizing..." James stopped and contemplated his own words before he continued, "Did you grow up in Birmingham?"

"Yes, I did... well the suburbs mostly, but yes, all my life."

"So, this was before your time, but you've probably read about it. There were a lot of protest all over the south... the country really... but Birmingham was kind of the center of it all. On the day I ended up here, a bomb had gone off at a church and all kinds of chaos ensued throughout the city. Four little girls were killed in the blast and a lot more hurt and probably died later but I don't know... we got reports of another kid being shot and killed across town and then heard that the police had killed another young man. Things were getting really crazy, and I had to be back in Nashville the next morning at 6 AM for my first rotation. My uncle was driving in from Chilton County to pick me up and drive me, but he didn't show up probably because of all the commotion in town. I called my aunt and he left on time, but she didn't know where he was or what had happened. I told Reverend Shuttlesworth, and he gave me thirty dollars to get a greyhound but warned me to be careful. Before I even got the station these four white guys started following me, so I turned toward southside to see if they were actually following me and they were. I zig zagged through the city and ended up on Morris and they started closing in, so I started running and they did too. They were about a block behind me when I went in that door," he said shaking his head. "That made a bad day worse. I should have just stood my ground. I'd probably be dead but sometimes I think that might be better than this."

"Oh, man, I'm sorry that happened. Yes, I know all about the bombing and the civil rights protests. It took way longer than it should have but you should know your work was not in vain. The church and several blocks around it were recently designated as a National Park. The park across from the church is now filled with sculptures honoring the protestors, foot soldiers, and leaders and those four little girls. And, on the block down from the church stands the Birmingham Civil Rights Institute and museum."

"Are you serious?" James had a look of total disbelief at this news, which for a man that has time traveled is saying a lot.

"The KKK members that bombed the church were finally prosecuted decades later... some had died before things changed enough to get them, but they paid. Birmingham elected a black mayor in the late seventies and has pretty much had a predominantly black city council and a black mayor since. A lot of things have changed. Mostly for the better but racial issues are still very prevalent, I'm sorry to say."

James was smiling and shaking his head trying to digest all the information.

"Thank you for telling me this. Ever since that day, I have thought about those little girls and all those folks I left behind. I figured in that chaos no one ever missed me, and things probably went back to the way they had been for so long. Of course, I was consumed with all this," he said waving his hands about, "but I think about those folks every day."

"Well, a lot of good changes have come about, but the world is still an ugly place at times," Sam said as he reached out and placed a consoling hand on James's knee.

James placed his hand on Sam's and peered into his eyes. "As bad as it was then, it's a lot worse in this time... I have come to appreciate those who came before me," he said with deep sadness in his voice and Sam could see it in his face.

"Yes, the treatment of people of color and women has been the biggest shock to me," Sam agreed. "In 2022, we have a black woman serving as Vice-President of the United States."

This news sent James reeling back in the chair. "A black woman... Vice President!" was all he could mutter as the smile returned to his face.

"Yes, she had served as the Senator from California for years and we had a black man as President for two terms before her," Sam added.

James was now beaming again. "Oh, I have got to get back so I can see this for myself!"

"So, you were a doctor then but now you're a blacksmith?"

"Yes. It was hard enough being a black doctor in 1963... it's impossible in 1901! I am lucky to be a blacksmith... probably wouldn't be if I wasn't able to use my knowledge in medicine to save a horse when I first got here, and Mr. Horton has been pretty decent to me... I get $10 a month and this place to stay," he said.

"Man, that sucks... I mean not getting to practice... I know things are so crude in this time and you could do so much."

"I could, but it is also so much more dangerous for me, so I have to be careful. That is why I talk the way I do... to them, I mean... the folks that took me in warned me that first day, an uppity-talking nigger would end up hanging from

69

the first tree they could find, so I adapted. I grew up in the country before coming to Birmingham to stay with my aunt and uncle at age 11. So, my medical skills are reserved for horses and donkeys... and even then, I am careful about what I do and what I say."

"So, you came here, and no one knew you or anything, right?" Sam asked.

"Correct."

"Well, I show up with this badge on my chest, not that I noticed it at first, but then I find out folks are expecting me! I have a letter from President Roosevelt appointing me Marshall here. The Chief of Police was expecting my arrival on the afternoon train the day I landed out there in the street and over the past month, I have pieced together some background of having served as a Deputy Marshal for the last nine years in Kentucky and Tennessee. I was convinced that I had a head injury, and my memory of the future was some crazy psychosis or something."

"That is strange and certainly different from my experience," James said absorbing Sam's story.

"Oh, and by the way... in 2022, I am 58 years old and now, by all accounts I am 32 and I look like I did in my thirties except for the weird clothes."

"I was 24 in 1963 and I have no idea how old I am here... I do look a bit younger; I think... but certainly not like your difference. I am much fitter than I was then though."

"So, it seems that other than both of us starting at the same point and landing in the same point, nothing else is the same," Sam said. "Let's think about specifics... times, dates, and such, to see if anything else synchs."

"I remember time travel being mentioned in a quantum physics class once, but it was basically unproven and just a lot of loose theories that had gone unproven for centuries... I have racked my brain for the last two years trying to come up with an answer," James said.

"I left 2022 on October 28 somewhere around 8:45 in the morning and landed here about twelve hours later in time... minus the 121 years," Sam said.

"I left 1963 a little after five in the evening of September 15 and landed here on that same date in 1899... about midnight or a little before as best I can tell... like I said, I was so rattled I walked around the city for a few hours, and I met the folks that took me in about daybreak."

"So, help me with my math... my travel was 121 years and took about 12 hours. Yours was 64 years and took maybe 7 hours or so... maybe there is some significance to that."

"Maybe," James answered though he didn't seem convinced. Sam was standing now and pacing in the small room.

"Wait! You left on September 15, 1963, around five?"

"Yes. I left the church around 4:45 to go catch the bus that left at 5:15 but didn't make it so I would say I went through the door sometime between 4:55 an 5:15 if that is important." James stopped because Sam had stopped pacing and looked as though he had seen a ghost. "What is it, man?"

"I was born on September 15, 1963, at 5:02 PM," he said, as his mind tried to fit that piece into the bizarre puzzle.

"Oh, my," was all James could say as both men sat in silence for the next several minutes digesting the information both had shared and contemplating how it all related.

Finally, Sam remembered the full moon that had provided a renewed hope for this evening. "Was the moon full that night?' he asked.

James thought for a moment. "I'm not sure about 1963... it was just getting dark and with all the tall buildings, I can't say... but, when I landed here it was full and bright."

"Well, that is another thing in common," Sam said as his mind tried to process all the information between the two.

The men talked for another three hours and agreed to meet as often as they could to continue their discussions and investigation, if you could call it that. James warned that they had to be careful because a white and black man could not be seen as too friendly, even if one was a U.S. Marshal. Sam reluctantly agreed and he understood. James reached out for a handshake as they reached the door. Sam took his hand, and then he embraced the muscular man in a bear hug.

"In 2022, men can hug... even men of different races," he smiled.

"Thank you," James replied as he unlatched the door and Sam slipped out into the night.

Chapter 8

For the next several weeks James and Sam discreetly met as often as they could and while no closer to finding a way home, they learned a lot about each other and their lives in their own times before ending up here in this time. They discussed all they knew about time travel which was a short conversation. Sam explained the premise of the Stephen King novel and didn't realize the significance of the date and title, *11/22/63*, until he saw the look on James's face. The JFK assassination occurred two months after he went through the door. There was a lot of history to fill in with more assassinations and political upheaval to explain. It was a fictional story, but the historical context was real. Too real for James. After many hours of discussion, both men were finally convinced that their story was real too. Neither held on to the hope that it was all just a dream. They were not sure how, but the fabric of time had wrinkled, and they both ended up in this time, but they felt there had to be some reason for it even if it was beyond their understanding.

Other than starting and landing in the same point years apart under a full moon, they could find no other similarities and they had certainly not found a way to go back through. If there was such a way, they hadn't found it yet, but each man held out hope that just as they landed here by chance, that some way they would also find their way back.

Sam kept a journal of the facts from each of their stories. The dates they went through the door, the day they landed, the time difference of their journeys. The only fact that seemed relevant to each was the door under the viaduct and landing at the same point earlier in time before the bridge was constructed, and the full moon.

The other glaring thing that could not be ignored was that James went through the door at or very near the exact time that Sam was born. *Coincidence? In this bizarre set of facts, who could say?*

The men continued their lives in this new world by day and tried to meet at least twice a week in James's room at the blacksmith shop. James went about his work as a blacksmith and carefully tending to horses with his medical training while being careful to not overstep his place in a hardline Jim Crow society. He kept his head down and his mouth shut and longed for his meetings with Sam where he could speak freely and learn about all the things the world had revealed after that fateful day in 1963.

Sam went about his duties as Marshal and tried to learn more about his past here. Through records and reports, he learned that he had joined the marshal service at the age of 20 in Bardstown, Kentucky and served as a deputy there for three years before being reassigned to Hazard, a coal mining town for three years and then briefly to Chattanooga, Tennessee before being sent to

Nashville for a short time before receiving the appointment in Birmingham.

Sam hoped that if he could figure out his own past here, he could figure out how he existed in this time as well in the 21st century. Each man hoped that something in his past would lead to an answer to get back home.

With James, it was as if he disappeared from 1963 and reappeared in 1899, but Sam seemed to have already been here before he was aware. *How does that corelate to everything else?* It was a dilemma that there were no answers for, at least no answers that Sam knew where to look.

He did figure out the early warnings he received from Chief Austin about the motives of men seeking to bring him to Birmingham. It seems that all were indeed politicians, including Chief Conrad Austin, although he had served as a police officer and Deputy Sherriff before being elected to the office of Police Chief. Sam thought about the bureaucracy and politics that made him eager to retire from the department when he had his 25 years in. *It was bad enough to have a chief appointed by the mayor, it would have probably been worse to have one elected every two years. It would be one continuous election cycle.* That is the main reason he never applied for the Sherriff's Department; your boss had to stand for election every four years.

Sam learned that earlier this year before his arrival, Chief Austin had garnered hero status by capturing a group of robbers known widely as the Miller-Duncan gang. The men had terrorized the south for years. In March the gang robbed the Standard Oil Company in Birmingham and killed two police officers who attempted to arrest them.

They were the first officers to die in the line of duty in the city. Austin led officers in pursuit, capturing both Miller and Duncan that same night and five other gang members in the coming weeks. The outlaws were now housed in a Montgomery jail awaiting trial.

He learned from his conversations with Austin that he was a progressive thinker for his time and had parlayed the murder of the officers into adding more policemen to the force, although they were still understaffed for the growing population. He also had just instituted the Bertillon System of recording physical details of every person arrested and other innovative record keeping methods that would set the foundation for modern police work. Although trend setting for the time, Sam winced at the archaic systems without fingerprints, photographs, or DNA.

He learned that Austin and Mayor Drennen were both newly elected in 1899. Both men were progressive for their time and were implementing policies and procedures that would help Birmingham grow as a city. He learned quickly that Austin, Drennen, Alderman George Ward, and Jefferson County Sherriff Frank O'Brien were all shrewd politicians of the time and used the police department, and law enforcement in general, as pillars of their campaigns. With elections occurring every two years they seemed to always be campaigning.

Emil Lesser and Paul Gilardoni were also rumored to be candidates but neither man had made any formal announcement. The liquor laws, Sunday Blue laws, and other ordinances governing civil behavior seemed to top everyone's list of campaign rhetoric, although most, if not all, had ownership in one or more saloons or similar enterprises, which made Sam think something was amiss although he had not put his finger on it just yet. If he could figure out how to get back to 2022, he wouldn't have to deal with it at all.

Sam knew that prohibition would come in the next decades and it would get much uglier before then, but he also knew that the rampant gambling and saloons that made his city feel like the wild west would also need to be curbed for a civilized city to emerge. None of this fit into his duty as U.S. Marshal but rather fell to local law enforcement, but when federal prohibition came in the next decade, it would fall in his lap, and he hoped he would be long gone before then.

The entire state seemed to be relieved that the new state constitution had finally been passed. The new document became effective on November 21, 1901, and had been years in the making laying the groundwork for many of the racist Jim Crow laws that would survive well into the next century. The document set out to undo any progressive statues from the brief reconstruction period after the Civil War. It contained more than 388,000 words and was by far the longest state constitution and was 51 times longer than the U.S. Constitution. Sam lamented to James that the ancient document was still the governing document of the state in 2022 with now almost 1,000 amendments making it much longer and even more cumbersome.

The entire city was mesmerized as the ten-story Woodward Building rose from the ashes on the southwest corner of 1st Avenue and 20th Street next door to the new Metropolitan Hotel. Sam had always been amused at the four buildings on the

77

corner being referred to as skyscrapers but looking at the 10-story building going up in the city, he finally understood. The massive structure would be the tallest building in Alabama and would soon dwarf the other buildings in Birmingham. It seemed so much bigger in this context than he remembered.

Sam watched each day as the building grew upward and men on simple scaffolds laid the brick façade around the iron skeleton. No high-rise cranes and special equipment, just sheer manpower and ingenuity. The foundations were being laid when he arrived and now four months later five-stories were complete, and the skeleton was up for the rest. Sam admired the ornate iron staircases with marble treads and oak paneling going in, knowing that these treasures would still be there in 2022. He also knew that in the next few years a taller building would be built on each corner of the intersection surpassing the previous one as the tallest, but he desperately hoped to be back to 2022 before those were here.

Despite the marvel of the Magic City literally rising around him, life in 1901 was hard, especially for a man born in the twentieth century when luxuries that had not yet come to fruition here were commonplace. Yet, as hard as life was for him, Sam knew that James had it much harder. Sam told James of the many advances of his race in the later twentieth century which seemed to make him forget his plight for the moment at least.

Sam showed James an article in the morning paper announcing that a group of citizens led by several women had purchased the 600 block of 20th Street South and planned to erect a new building for the Hillman Hospital that had been operating in an old house in the city for four years. He told him that the building still stood in 2022 and was now surrounded by the sprawling medical center at UAB that now occupied much of the city's south side and was often recognized as one of the top medical centers in the world.

They also talked about the lack of progress in race relations that was, no doubt, deeply rooted in the systems and practices that were underway during this time, further complicated by the new state constitution. In the years following the civil war, reconstruction efforts showed great promise for a bright future but soon men – white men – found ways to circumvent and ignore laws desperately trying to return the south to a time when they controlled everything. The federal government was complicit in this fearing another uprising and so Jim Crow laws became the norm and citizens of color were relegated to a second-class status or worse. The 1901 Alabama Constitution would solidify many of those Jim Crow laws for decades to come.

The men often discussed their similar paths to this time but also tried to dissect the differences in their plights. After weeks of discussions, their theory was that James also likely had a back story, but as a black man, there were no records and in society at that time, a black person was dispensable, so unless he happened upon someone who knew him or family, they would likely never know what that history was.

Sam had tried to find any family he may have had reaching out to former colleagues in Kentucky, but the inquiries had to be delicate. You had to be careful asking questions that you should already know the answers to. He determined that he had no close family and had been taken in by a local Sheriff as a teen which was his pathway into law enforcement. The sheriff had been killed in the line of duty while Sam was assigned in Tennessee. Other than that, he had hit dead ends and nothing pointed to any cosmic revelation of his landing in 1901 or how his birth coinciding with James going through the door fit into all this but he felt there had to be a connection somehow.

As Christmas approached again, Sam had now spent more than a year and James more than three years trapped in this time. Although they continued to meet at least twice a week, their conversations now rarely discussed ways of escape anymore. They had simply talked the subject to death and had no real clues as to how this happened or how to reverse it. For months they searched for an invisible portal on or near the spot that they both landed but there was nothing. Nothing but the cobblestone street and buildings. No portal. No magic. No way back. So, the men spent their visits in conversation and sometimes in the silent company of the only person that could understand their predicament.

Sam learned that James had been engaged to marry Alma Johnston the summer before he left for medical school in Nashville. The two had met during his freshman year at Alabama State University in Montgomery. She was a junior from

Birmingham and the two became friends on bus rides back home on breaks.

Alma became a teacher in the colored high school in Birmingham following her graduation and James came to visit on every break when he could find a way up from Montgomery.

Alma's family was very active in the civil rights movement and by the time James had been accepted in the medical school at Meharry Medical College in Nashville, the two were planning a life together. They married before he headed off to Med school and she supported them with her teaching job in Birmingham and they saved money by her staying with her parents.

James revealed that he was holding out hope that the part of the Stephen King novel about only losing two minutes in time no matter how long you were in the past was true. Before Sam came along, he had tried to forget about Alma but that was not possible. He missed her every day and since learning of what the future would bring, he longed even more to spend those decades with her.

Sam often thought of Joan and what she might make of all this. She had a passion for history and would probably love the things he was experiencing. He just longed for a hot shower and cold beer and TV. He missed TV.

By the time summer rolled around, Sam had gained a reputation around town for his level head and fair dealings. Not being in a constant campaign status set him apart from the local government establishment, especially with the other cops. The city was growing so fast, even with constant new hires, the force was woefully understaffed, and Sam helped whenever he could.

William Wier, a former Captain in the department had been elected as Police Chief in the recent election. Conrad Austin now managed the Commercial Detective Bureau, a private agency that occupied offices on the 5th floor of the Jefferson Bank building on 2nd Avenue North. Sam kept in touch with the man that seemed to be relieved to put politics behind him.

Sam's most interesting meeting since his arrival came late in the summer when a young man came to his office asking if the Marshal could see him. Charles sent the short, well-dressed young man back to Sam.

Thomas Motlow explained to Sam that he was a student at Vanderbilt University in Nashville and was spending the summer in Birmingham on behalf of his older brothers and uncle. He explained that his uncle, Jack Daniels, operated a distillery in their hometown of Lynchburg, Tennessee and that his brothers had been operating saloons in Gadsden, Alabama for a few years and were hoping to find a suitable place in the booming city of Birmingham to establish their own distilling business. He explained that he had learned the marshal was a fair man and despite the growing resentment of saloons and such businesses would provide a fair assessment of whether such a business venture might be feasible in this town.

Sam almost choked when the lad threw out his famed uncle's name but was able to recover without being too obvious. He told young Thomas that he was sworn to uphold the law and had no control over the changing tide but could assure him that unless laws were passed to prohibit its operation that he could see no barriers if the company abided by both local and federal laws. The young man thanked Sam and shook his hand. "If you are a whiskey drinker, I will bring you a bottle of Uncle's number 7 when I come back to town. It's the finest around," he said as he left.

Sam sat back in his chair and lost himself in the memory of the time he and Joan toured the Lynchburg distillery on their way home from a trip Gatlinburg. *Unbelievable!*

This was the second historical meeting Sam had encountered this summer. A few weeks earlier on his daily walks through downtown he noticed that one of the saloons that lined the east side of 24th Street between 1st and 2nd Avenue North was being emptied of its furnishings as a man oversaw the goods being loaded onto a wagon. The man introduced himself to the marshal as Crawford Johnson. He explained that the former saloon would be the headquarters for his new business. He told Sam that he had recently purchased the bottling rights from the Chattanooga Coca-Cola Bottling Company and was establishing the Birmingham Coca-Cola Bottling Company.

"Prohibition is coming," he explained. "Sooner or later in some form or fashion, but it is coming. Our drink is refreshing and contains no alcohol."

Sam dropped in on Mr. Johnson the following week and met his sole employee, a black man who was also known as Sam, and Sara, the mule that pulled the wagon. Sam was an older man with strong shoulders, graying hair, and a quiet disposition. The marshal tried to joke with him about their shared name, but either it didn't register with the man, or he was afraid to be seen in conversation with the marshal. Or it could be that he was just too busy for conversation. The other Sam and Sara were delivering the new concoction as fast as they could make it. By the end of the year the business had grown, and Mr. Crawford had hired several more employees and the small former saloon was a hive of activity. Sam overheard the saloon keeper on the corner of 1st Avenue claim that Crawford had to hire three men just to count the money coming in every day!

As Sam sat there thinking of these two encounters, he could not help but think about Jack and Coke, a simple cocktail that was known world-wide in 2022. *What are the chances!*

As Christmas approached again, Sam and James continued their weekly meetings in the shop. It had been months since either man spoke of returning to the lives they once knew. They did swap stories of Christmases growing up and dinners with families and friends.

Two weeks earlier, Sam had arranged for Paul to prepare a small Thanksgiving dinner in a wicker basket, and he had surprised James with a meal of fried chicken, mashed potatoes, and green beans. The two men sat in the sparse room in the back of the shop and shared the meal on the rickety table in the glow of the lantern.

Tonight, Sam had brought pork chops with gravy and potatoes. The food was much simpler than the food that was being dished up in the numerous restaurants that lined almost every street in town in 2022, but it was delicious and made Sam long for home.

The men had a brief discussion of the ongoing politics in town. James was very aware of all the current events even though he was not allowed to vote and had to be careful to read the newspapers in private. The wrong people knowing that he could read might bring trouble so he avoided it as best he could. There was always news of the crime affiliated with the saloons and drunken miners in town on the weekends. It always accompanied a story or two about the understaffed police force. The big push was for Birmingham to incorporate all the surrounding municipalities into one city. Greater Birmingham was the most common reference made to bring in the towns of Avondale, Woodlawn, and others into the city. Like beefing up the police force, all the politicians were for the idea, but varied greatly on how to do it and how to fund it. Most knew that it would come at some point, but the city was still growing so fast that it was difficult to comprehend expanding the borders and annexing thousands of more citizens at once and the politicians weren't sure what that might bring.

Sam knew that it must eventually come into being because all the city neighborhoods he was familiar with in his time were now separate cities. The city of North Birmingham had just been incorporated earlier in the year.

Although they rarely spoke about it anymore, Sam could not help but make a slow walk along Morris every time there was a full moon. Somewhere in the deep recess of his mind he hoped to stumble through an invisible portal to reemerge in 2022 but so far that had not happened. The only thing he stumbled over was the occasional pile of horse shit in the street.

As Christmas arrived again the men shared another meal that Sam brought in. There was a bit of stories of their youth, but the occasion weighed heavy, and they mostly ate in silence. 1903 was about to arrive and despite the everchanging city around them, both men were resolved that not much would change in their lives. Sam tried to convince James that with his help he could emerge and use his skills and knowledge as a physician, but James knew better. Sam knew that it was ultimately James's decision to make but hated seeing his friend miserable; but really, they were both miserable. During their many discussions they had decided on a quirky sign that each man could use in public to let the other know that they needed to talk. Sam had told James about his favorite movie as a kid, *The Sting*, and the signal that Paul Newman and Robert Redford used. A simple finger beside the nose that would go unnoticed by anyone else but would signal each other of the need to meet. So far nothing had ever come up that could not wait until their weekly meeting but the two saw each other almost every day in passing.

After their meal, they shared a prolonged bear hug before Sam slipped out the door into the chill of the night.

Chapter 9

As the New Year of 1903 ushered in new buildings and even more activity downtown, Sam was no more resolved in this life than he had been and still longed for his convenient life in 2022. He and James seemed to try harder to encourage each other at their weekly meetings but with each fleeting week it seemed to grow harder to do so. The daily grind along with no hope to return were ever present.

Sam always felt a tinge of guilt for he knew his plight, as rough as it was, was so much better than James's. Not only because he was a white man and a U.S. Marshal, but because he had not left behind a wife and family. He tried to console himself with that, but it was really easy to sink into a pity party. As the weeks passed, he thought less and less about the future that was his past and just tried to live in the day.

As a young man with no family, he had been introduced to a number of eligible young ladies that batted their eyes at the tall lawman, but Sam avoided the situations whenever possible. Luckily, most families were not all that anxious to marry off their daughters to a lawman that may or may not have a long-life expectancy. Sam was happy with that and anytime he felt drawn to relieve his manly desires in one of the many brothels in town, he had only to remember the absence of any antibiotics to quell the longing. Celibacy seemed the only answer. It wasn't that he didn't have desires. He was a widow and with this transformation he was a young man in his prime, but regardless of how he looked and felt physically, he still felt like the 58-year-old man that he was. Not that he didn't have desires too, but he wasn't ready for that just yet. He looked at the young ladies he met and felt even more like he would be an old man preying on the young. Regardless of his looks, he was still that mature man inside.

He and Joan had shared thirty-four years of wedded bliss. She was his lover, his best friend, and he although he had grieved and felt like he had moved on, he wasn't ready to move on in that regard.

He was often invited to social gatherings with the movers and shakers in the city but tried to avoid them whenever possible because they always ended up in some political drama that he wanted no part of. He had made some friends outside the political spectrum in town. His closest friends were the young female doctor and a friend of hers. The three of them settled into a routine of having dinner almost every week. They also attended shows and operas in town whenever they could.

Dr. Irene Bullard, despite being a woman, had a very successful medical practice. She saw a number of patients each day in her small office in the Watts Building and, on several evenings, made quiet visits to many of the brothels in town to tend to the various needs of the women there. Her friend, Dr. Tom Thaxton, was a dentist whose primary practice was in the mining town of Pratt City, a few miles west of Birmingham. Tom had recently set up an office down the hall from Irene and saw patients there two days each week. Despite both being healthcare professionals, Sam found the pair to be an odd couple. After a few weeks of dinner meetings, he was sure the relationship was strictly platonic. They seemed more like proper siblings than work colleagues and they both seemed to be at ease with Sam which was unusual. Law enforcement types have a hard time fitting in in modern times, much less in the Victorian era society of the day.

Birmingham was a melting pot of all types. The city had immigrants flooding in for the opportunities the new city offered. There were Italians, Germans, Scots, and Irish. Along with the Anglo-Saxons that had been born here, the descendants of immigrants from various countries, they filled every level of the social ladder. There were miners and steel workers, of course, but there were also merchants, bankers, jewelers, and saloon keepers... lots of saloon keepers.

Irene had grown up in New York and her family had moved south to care for her aging grandparents when she was in college. She was the only female in her class at the Syracuse Medical School and decided to move to the south to start her practice. She was determined to overcome the odds and it appeared she was succeeding.

Dr. T.T. (Tom) Thaxton had grown up in south Alabama and had settled in the Birmingham area after completing dental school, landing in Pratt City, a thriving industrial city just a short train ride from Birmingham. With the boom going on in Birmingham, he was considering a move into the city.

After getting to know the pair, Sam secretly decided that one or both may be gay. It was something that was not even hinted at during that era, so he couldn't be sure. Sam had plenty of gay friends in 2022 but had been old enough to see the coming of age for the LGBTQ community during and after the AIDS Crisis. Everything in this era was so buttoned up, even for heterosexual couples, he could not imagine what being gay in 1903 would encompass. He enjoyed the social meetings and conversations with his new friends and although he was initially attracted to the young doctor, there was never any hint of romance or anything other than friendship.

The three met each Thursday for dinner and conversation and that was that. Sam enjoyed talking about anything that didn't involve work and that gave him some escape. They even attended an occasional opera, play or other musical performances beginning to appear at the theatres popping up in the city. It was a welcomed relief from the monotony for Sam. He missed his downtown loft friends. He missed dinners and concerts. He missed 2022.

Tonight's dinner conversation centered around the news stories of the day that the Birmingham Commercial Club had commissioned Italian sculptor, Giuseppe Moretti, to create an iron statue to be displayed at the 1904 World's Fair in St. Louis, Missouri. It was the consensus opinion that if they could pull it off, it would definitely put the city on the map and open up the eyes of many about the potential the city held. It was hard for Sam to hold back about the famed symbol of his beloved city that had stood atop Red Mountain overlooking the city for his entire life. He had grown up visiting Vulcan Park every time an out of town relative visited. He had Joan had frequently visited the statue's observation deck overlooking the city below. It made for an expensive date when they were poor college students. He had worn an image of the statue on his shoulder as a police officer for 25 years as it was the prominent figure in the patch on every uniform. But he sat and speculated with Irene and Tom as to how Giuseppe Moretti could possibly pull off the feat in such a short time.

The city was changing daily it seemed, as opera houses and theatres brought national acts to welcoming audiences but there was also an escalation in burlesque and other bawdy acts too. The saloons were booming and there was never a shortage of drama. For the most part, Sam was able to stay out of the fray, leaving the chaos to the city police officers to handle. But on occasion he had been drawn into a fist fight or two. Robberies and thefts were almost commonplace but like in the 21st century, the criminal element was usually not very smart and were often caught on the spot. Sam had already had to pull his sidearm more in the last two years than he had in his entire career as an officer or Deputy Marshal. Thankfully, he had not had to fire it yet, but that all changed on his way home from dinner that night.

Sam said his farewells to the doctors and then made his way from the restaurant on 2nd over to Morris for his stroll back to the hotel. As he made his way up 24th Street to the corner of 1st Avenue, a crowd was gathered on the sidewalk in front of the Manhattan Saloon. Soon, two Birmingham Policemen came out through the crowd, each one dragging a nearly unconscious man and dropped the pair on the sidewalk to catch their breath. Officer Ted Wharton noticed Sam observing.

"Drunken card cheats, Marshal!" he said still gasping for air.

Once he could talk, the officer explained that a fight had broken out upstairs when the two miners accused each other of cheating and the police were summoned when a knife was drawn. When they arrived, the pair decided to team up to take on the cops, but they were quickly subdued. As the wagon arrived and the two thugs were hoisted in, the crowd dispersed, most back inside the busy saloon.

While gambling was illegal, many of the saloons held space in their upstairs for those guests that wanted to partake in such vices. Generally, the police ignored them as long as they otherwise behaved. The undermanned force had more pressing duties. That was until it was near election time, then the Sheriff and Police Chief made a point of informing the citizen of their all-out efforts to rid the city of such heinous debauchery by conducting frequent raids. The savvier saloon keepers would normally just cease operations until the election was decided before resuming the games. The operator of the Saloon and Pool Hall two blocks west had addressed the issue by simply removing the stairs to the second floor. Patrons entered the gaming establishment via a ladder, in the alley, that was lowered on their approval to enter. Cops coming to raid the place would have to bring their own ladder providing plenty of time to cease the games and hide the evidence. It was a brilliant solution Sam thought.

After the ruckus was over, Sam continued his stroll crossing 1st Avenue and down to Morris. The cobblestone lane was eerily quiet, and Sam couldn't help but think of that first night he woke up lying in the middle of the street. He tried not to think about that night these days, but he still walked by the spot every night. He hoped that one night a miracle would happen, and he would be transported back to 2022. It was a crazy thought, but his being here now was crazy too.

As Sam approached 21st Street he noticed the glimmering reflection on the blacksmith shop door ahead. *James must be working late.* As he stepped off the sidewalk to cross the street, he sensed movement in the shadows between the buildings where James had scared the shit out him the night he revealed his secret. Sam froze in the middle of the street as three figures emerged onto the sidewalk. It was not a full moon tonight, so the shadows were heavy and only pierced by the glow of the new streetlamp on the corner. The men stopped on the sidewalk, and each stood about six feet apart. Sam wasn't sure, but their body language told him they were not there to ask him how his dinner was. Sam slowly walked up the middle of the vacant street never taking his eyes off the trio. As he got closer his suspicions were confirmed. Each man wore a sidearm and the one to his far right carried a long gun in his hands. Then the middle man broke the silence.

"You Marshal Robbins?" he asked in a deep southern baritone.

"I am... who's asking?" Sam replied sternly while running a gamut of reaction scenarios through his brain depending on what move they made. His years of training had prepared him for all sorts of confrontations and situations, but a Matt Dillion three on one draw-down in the middle of the street was not among them.

"You 'member our daddy, Harlan Hill?" the man asked, his voice cracking ever so slightly.

Sam felt the chill run up his spine at that name. *Of course, I remember the bastard... he almost killed me! But that was in 2012... what the hell?*

The men didn't wait for an answer. Sam saw the man pulling his weapon from the holster on his right side followed a nano-second later by his brother on the left. The brother on the right was raising the shotgun and the conversation had come to a quick end as Sam drew his Colt and fired striking the middle man in the chest as he heard the lead whiz by his left ear from the muzzle flash of the left brother's gun and he fired again. Before the flash from his own gun cleared, he saw the shotgun skitter across the cobblestones as that brother went flying backwards. Sam's second bullet found its target in the left brother's chest as he fell backward, his gun firing again upward into the gray sky as he landed hard on the sidewalk. Sam could now see behind where the shotgun man had been standing and saw James with a long leather whip as the man recovered and drew his sidearm and pointed it at the hulking black man just six feet in front of him. He never got the shot off as Sam fired a round in the side of his face making a mess on the brick wall behind him. James stood in shock and then ran to the other two men sprawled on the street and sidewalk. There was no helping the shotgun man with the missing face, but the doctor had to check on the other two even if they had just tried to kill his friend. Both men were dead, a bloody hole in the center of each one's chest. Sam was still standing in the middle of the street, his Colt in his right hand dangled by his side, staring at the carnage before him.

"You alright, Sam?" James called out.

"I think so," Sam said snapping back to reality that was too surreal to be considered reality.

As Sam walked over to stare at the bodies, he saw the concern in his friend's eyes.

"What the hell happened?" James asked as he carefully looked Sam over for injuries.

"Not sure... but I am glad you were here," he said as the gravity of the event still hadn't quite implanted in his brain.

"I just happened to look out and I see you looking like a Wyatt Earp movie or something. Thought you might need some help, but I was not expecting that."

Sam heard sounds and looked to see several people coming down the street from both directions.

"Probably best if you slip back in the shop. I'll handle this," Sam said. "I will catch up later."

"Yep," was all James said as he disappeared into the black void between the buildings.

Sam kept the small crowd of onlookers at bay until the first police officers arrived moments later. Sam was glad to see one he knew. It was Ted Wharton. Soon Captain Andrew Marin arrived and took charge of the scene, directing officers to keep the crowd back and assigning other tasks before approaching Sam.

"You know who these men are, Marshall?"

"I was walking down the street and they stepped out of the shadows. Asked me if I knew their daddy, Harland Hill, and then drew their guns. I'm lucky. I felt one bullet whiz by my ear."

"Damn good shot," the captain quipped looking at the two bodies with gaping chest wounds before walking over to the crumpled corpse with the missing face. "What happened to this one?"

"Not sure. Dropped his shot gun and fell down when the shooting started," Sam answered pointing to the shotgun in the middle of the street. "Then he drew his sidearm and I had no choice."

The captain was now stooped over the corpse and struck a match to light the scene. "How did these cuts on his arms and neck happen?" he asked looking back at Sam.

Sam stepped in closer and could see the torn flesh across both arms and the left side of his neck where, no doubt, James's whip had landed.

"No idea. Must have happened before."

"Harland Hill, you say?" the captain asked, extinguishing the match, and dropping his curiosity of the corpse's wounds.

"Yes. He said, our daddy Harland Hill, so I guess they are brothers, maybe?"

"That name mean anything to you?"

"Not that I can think of, but I have arrested a lot of men in the last twelve years," Sam answered. He was not about to try an explain how Harland Hill had damn near shot his leg off in 2012 when Sam confronted him less than five blocks from this very spot.

Sam had responded to a call for back up at a pawn shop robbery on 1st Avenue North and 24th Street where three employees had been shot. The robber fled, but not before the owner had managed to shoot him in the ass as he neared the door.

As Sam approached the scene, he saw a tall white man emerge from behind a dumpster in the alley about a half block from the scene. He threw his spotlight on the man to see his jeans soaked in blood. Sam exited his car but before he could say anything a .44 caliber round tore through the cruiser's door and into his right thigh. Sam managed to draw his gun as he rolled over to see the man taking aim again. Sam put two 9mm rounds in his chest. Threat over. Harland Hill, a long-time felon, lay dead. Sam was cleared in the shooting and given a medal for his valor and was back on the job ten months later.

Is this another coincidence or is this another bizarre piece of the puzzle in this crazy time warp?

"I will check our records in the morning to see if that name comes up," Sam answered. "Do you need my gun?" he asked only to see the puzzled stare from the captain as the words left his mouth.

"No. I think you might need it." He said with a slight smile underneath the handlebar moustache. "The wagon will be here soon to get this cleaned up. I will check for a positive identification, but I am thinking that no one will miss these scoundrels."

Sam was anxious to check on James and to tell him about the uncanny development but knew that it would be far too risky tonight, so he headed to the hotel. The restaurant had closed but he spotted Paul cleaning up and asked if he could bother him for a drink. Sam sat at the bar and nursed a heavy pour of Mr. Daniel's finest Lincoln County corn whiskey and tried to unwind from what was now the most eventful night of his new existence. With each sip of the whiskey, he could smell the cordite fresh on his hand. In 2022 his weapon would have gone in an evidence bag and his hands thoroughly swabbed for evidence before sitting for hours of interrogating questions. He would have been on administrative leave for weeks while the shooting was investigated by Internal Affairs, the State Department of Public Safety, the District Attorney, and several other entities before he would be cleared to work again. Now he still had his gun and would go to work in the morning just like any other day.

The whiskey was beginning to take the edge off the adrenaline rush and Sam suddenly felt tired. A good night's sleep would be welcomed.

Chapter 10

Sleep came in small increments for Sam that night as he continually replayed the events that seemed more like a John Wayne movie than reality. *Was it reality? How do the sons of a thug I killed in 2012 show up in my 1903 nightmare?* Before the sun crept through the window, Sam had given up on sleep and settled on a long hot bath to start his day.

He made his way down the hall to the bathroom and drew a tub of hot water and eased his tired body in. His mind was still replaying last night's event as if it were a continuous loop, occasionally interrupted by the scene in the alley from 2012. As he ran the cake of soap over his body, he stopped at the scar just above his right knee. The 44-magnum slug from Harland Hill's hand cannon had shattered the bone and required two surgeries and lots of hardware to repair. The circular entry wound was surrounded by surgical incisions and numerous lines from the countless sutures. It was touch and go for more than a week on whether a skin graft would be required, but in the end, it would just be the ugly scars. As Sam rinsed the soap away, he noticed the scar was even uglier than he remembered, although slightly smaller. The surgical scars were not there. The circular scar was smaller and only showed signs of sutures on the perimeter. He felt the scar and it felt different too. *Well, it is certainly not the strangest thing that's happened to me. Not by a long shot!*

He got dressed and headed down for breakfast. There was no Twitter, Facebook, or Instagram but the word had spread already about the events of ten hours ago. It seemed everyone was aware of the shootout just down the street. A few folks showed genuine concern, but most were eager to give the Marshal praise for putting the bad guys away.

After breakfast, Sam headed straight to the office and began to dig through the reports he had accumulated over the last year as he tried to piece together a history on the Sam Robbins of this century. To the best of his memory there had been about a dozen or so times that he had discharged his weapon in the line of duty. A bank robbery in Louisville. A train robbery in Bardstown. A miner's strike that turned ugly in Hazard. He was shocked when he kept finding so many reports but often the details were sparse. He had been in a total of 13 gun battles and too many fights to count. He knew of at least 5 men that died from his hand but there were others with vague outcomes. Yet, there had been no investigations. Generally, the local authorities or coroner deemed the bad guys got what they deserved and that was that. He read back through each incident looking for details that he might have been missed. He was so absorbed with his research that he didn't hear Charles come in and almost jumped out his skin at the sound of his voice.

"Good morning! You are here early," Charles said from the doorway. "Sorry, I did not mean to startle you."

Sam recovered and tried to suck the air back in and hoped his reaction was not as bad as he thought it was. "Good morning, I had a long night," was all he could say before Charles chimed back in.

"Yes, I heard! Are you alright?" he asked and seemed genuinely concerned. "Is there anything I can help with?"

"Yeah, I'm okay considering," Sam answered shuffling the disarray of paper piles in front of him. "I am trying to see if I can find the name Harlan Hill in any of this," Sam explained gesturing to the mess on his desk. "They asked if I remembered their daddy, Harland Hill. I don't think they wanted an answer because they all drew down before I could even think."

"Hazard," Charles answered promptly. "Robbed a saloon, I believe."

Sam looked at the young man in amazement before digging for the Hazard, Kentucky stack of reports. About halfway down the stack was a report with name Harland Hill. It was a death report. Shot twice by Deputy Marshal Sam Robbins.

"I believe he shot you, didn't he?" Charles asked.

Sam was scanning the report and gasped when read that he had been wounded in the right leg before returning fire and killing the robber.

"Yes, that's right," Sam said hoping his total lack of knowing the story didn't show. "I never remember names," he said calmly trying to further cover his ignorance.

"You think it was his son's last night?" Charles asked.

"It would seem so. Not sure why it took them almost five years, but they seemed hell bent on finishing what their father started."

Sam spent the rest of the morning organizing the reports into incidents separated by time and location and filed them away in the empty file drawer in his desk.

As he started out for lunch, he was met in the hall just outside his offices by the mustached Captain Marin.

"You still working?" Sam asked surprised to see him still in uniform.

"No, I went home and got some sleep. How are you?"

"As well as can be expected. I found the name Harland Hill. I was just on my way down to report it," Sam said.

"Hazard, Kentucky?"

"Yes. How did you know?"

"One of my officers pulled a receipt from one their pockets with a Hazard address, so we telegraphed the Sherriff up there last night. Just got his reply. Seems the boys were wanted in a number of robberies from Ohio to Tennessee. We are still working on the details, but it looks like they got what they deserved."

"Well, the apple doesn't fall far... I killed their father in a saloon robbery five years back. Just didn't remember his name. He shot me in the leg."

"I will let you know when we get more information, but you did the world a good service last night, Marshal."

"I am just glad that no one else was hurt, including me."

"Oh, did you hear that Conrad's Father passed away?"

"No, I didn't. I will stop by his office to offer my condolences."

"Davis was a fine man. I think Conrad is down south helping with the arrangements, but he should be back next week."

"I will look in on him then. Thanks for letting me know."

Sam noted a spike in his notoriety at lunch and hoped that the admiration would wane soon. It was a bit uncomfortable being congratulated for taking the lives of three men, no matter how despicable they may have been. He desperately wanted to discuss the events with James but knew that would have to wait until after dinner. He couldn't help but wonder if the trio were also time traveling sons of the man from 2012. Or could he have now killed the same man twice in two different centuries? The coincident was too strong to ignore. The name. His bullet wound in the same place. In his quest for answers, it seemed that there were only more questions, each one more inexplicable than the one before it.

On his way to dinner, Sam strolled past the blacksmith shop and stopped across the street. He could see James working over the fire inside the door. When he looked up, Sam placed his finger beside his nose before continuing his walk. James responded with the slightest nod as he returned to his work.

Sam finished dinner and started his walk through town. The energy was high, and saloons were packed on this Friday night. It was payday for most of the workers and they all seemed anxious to spend it tonight. As Sam strolled through the city, he realized just how relaxed he had been prior to last night but that was over. His eyes darted to meet every movement and his senses were on high alert. It was like returning to work after his shooting in 2012. He never responded to a call the same after that. It was if your brain found another level of awareness and stayed on high alert all the time. As he turned on Morris, it was again eerily quiet. No work going in in the warehouses as all the workers were in the Saloons on 1st and 2nd Avenues. He stopped at the scene of last night's shootout. The only signs remaining was the faint stain on the brick wall and another on the sidewalk. He replayed the unreal scene in his mind and his heart raced again.

He made his way to the blacksmith shop and found the front doors shuttered. He walked to the back by the tracks and glanced around to make sure he was alone before knocking on the door. James opened the door and he slipped in. Sam handed James the sack filled with fried chicken, collards, and mashed potatoes from Paul's Café. His smile got even bigger as he peered into the bag and was hit with aroma of the warm food.

Sam filled James in on all the details since their parting last evening as James devoured the food. He was absorbing all the details until Sam dropped the fact that the reference to Harland Hill was a man he had killed in 2012 after the man shot him. James sat dumbfounded and then Sam dropped the fact that he had evidently also killed Harland Hill in 1898 after the man shot him in the same leg. James was sure he hadn't heard Sam correctly and asked that he repeat those facts for clarification. Sam told him all the details of the 2012 shootout in the alley and the complications incurred with the wound in his leg. As a doctor, James seemed to lock in on the modern medicine and asked more questions about the surgeries and treatment.

"That's fascinating," was all he could manage as Sam told him of the plate and screws implanted by surgeons to mend the shattered bone. "Would you mind if I take a look at the scar?"

Sam stood and put his right foot on the seat of the rickety chair and pulled his pant leg up as high as he could exposing the scar. James reached for the lantern on the wall and sat it on the edge of the table to illuminate the scar.

"That is some sloppy suturing," he said. "Certainly looks like something that would be done now... likely done in a hurry to close the wound. It looks as though this would have likely missed the femur. It may have nicked it but it's offline," he said looking at the exit wound on the back of his leg.

"In 2022, the bullet scar is about twice that big and more centered. And there are incision marks here and here," Sam explained pointing to the spots adjacent to the scar.

"This adds another big wrinkle in the time warp situation," James said as Sam let his pants leg unfurl and took his seat again. "Any thoughts?"

"I've been thinking about it all night and all I have are more questions. I remember 2012, of course, but I only have really sketchy handwritten reports of the incident in 1898," Sam said. "So, the only thing I know for sure is that a man named Harland Hill was the man who shot me, and I killed both times more than 100 years apart. No idea if they were the same man or not. I keep running scenarios through my brain. Was it the same guy trying to kill me in 1898 so I wouldn't kill him 2012? Or were those three last night from the future and came here looking for revenge or to kill me here so I couldn't kill their father in 2012? There are just too many crazy possibilities, especially since we have no idea how any of this works."

"I certainly don't have any answers. It seems every time we learn something it raises more questions and confusion," was all that James could offer.

"I guess I should be glad that it seems as though the investigation, if you can call it that, of last night's shooting is over. In 2022, I would be a miserable wreck for the next month while everybody and their brother delved into every aspect before deciding to clear it as justified or to send me to the pokey."

"So, it's cleared?"

"Seems so. It's like I am a hero or something. Evidently, that trio was wanted for a string of robberies from Ohio down through Tennessee. They killed at least four people in the process."

The men sat in silence for several minutes digesting the convoluted possibilities of the events more than a century apart. Finally, Sam was anxious to think about anything else and pointed to an article in the Birmingham Age Herald newspaper on the table.

"Looks like the Hillman Hospital will be opening soon," he said pointing to an article about the building nearing completion on the corner of 20th Street and Avenue F.

106

"Yes, I read that article and all I could think about was your description of how that building is now surrounded by skyscrapers for blocks and I tried to envision just what a 21st century medical center looks like."

"It is mind boggling in 2022 but when I look at that lone four-story building in that photo, it hits me even more. I know it was named after the head of Tennessee Coal and Iron, but do you know why? Money, I assume?"

"Yes. He donated lots of money to start the hospital with the condition that it be a charity hospital to take care of everyone -- poor and rich -- and black and white. He evidently made that a condition of the money, although you don't read about that part in the newspapers, but I heard some doctors and other folks talking about in here one day a few months ago."

The men spent another hour trying to talk about anything but time travels and their plight in this century, but it was always hanging there. They shared a hug, and both looked forward to meeting again next week.

Sam slipped out the door to the clanging rhythm of two trains moving slowly down the tracks in opposite directions. He made his way back out to Morris and could not help but stare at the spot where he had awakened almost two years ago. How could that possibly be explained? Then his gaze traveled about thirty yards down the street to where he stood last night, and the scene replayed in his mind again. He walked down the sidewalk and stood looking at the faint traces of the man's blood embedded in the brick wall and sidewalk. He looked to the street where he had stood. It was less than twenty feet away. A blast from the shotgun would have definitely ended him. James had saved his life and as much as he wanted to them both to be home, he was thankful that his friend was looking out for him last night.

Chapter 11

The remainder of 1903 was less eventful after that night and after a few weeks, Sam and James had once again grown weary and stopped trying to decipher what it all meant. There were no answers. Only more questions.

Sam had tried to get more details on the 1898 version of Harland Hill but got little information and none that helped with the time puzzle. Harland's oldest son was part of the gang when Sam had killed Harland in the attempted robbery. The two younger sons joined in after their father's death, even though the youngest was only fifteen at the time. He was the shotgun man the night of the confrontation and barely twenty years old.

Sam and James both tried to settle back into their respective routines and continued to meet at least once a week. As before, their conversations about that night, and time travel in general, soon faded. It was just too painful unless they talked about some advancement that came about after James went through the door that could lift spirits and provide a topic of conversation for the night. They usually stayed with topics of the day. It was less painful for them both.

1904 came in hard with an eight-inch snowfall on January 28th. Sam found that the south was no better prepared for such an event than they were a hundred years later. Luckily the snow melted within a few days and things got back to somewhat normal.

Buildings were still popping up all over town. Each one seemed to be taller and more ornate than its predecessor. Mining and steel production was also booming feeding the growth as more companies sprang up or relocated to the Magic City to take advantage of the growing opportunities. The workforce was fed by a constant stream of immigrants from across the globe as well as farmers deciding that mining or steel making could provide a much more stable income than farming. They moved into the city from across the south and Midwest.

Sam had now been here for thirty-nine months and most days it seemed more like forever. He tried to stay occupied serving papers and helping out the police department whenever he was asked. He had exhausted his search for clues on his own past and had turned to looking for any history tied to James which proved to be even more frustrating. A black man in 1904 was not entered in most records except for arrest records and it appeared that James had a clean record. Sam had even taken a train south to the town of Verbena in Chilton County about sixty miles south of Birmingham. The sleepy town was where most of James's family resided in the 20th century where they farmed the land for several generations. It was a long shot, but it was all Sam had to go on and he did not turn up any leads.

In 1904, the town was more of a resort area or travel stop with two hotels, a bank, a post office, and a large general store. He could find no one named Lewis in the area, but someone told him that a family by the name of Johnston had lived there a short time before moving to Birmingham. Sam had no idea if those Johnstons were any kin to James's wife but at least it was something to follow up on. When he returned to Birmingham, he had no luck locating the Johnston family.

Other than his conversations with James, Sam's only joy came from his regular outings to the theatre and concerts. He continued to meet Drs. Burton and Thaxton for dinner at least twice a month and continued to attend theatrical shows and events with the odd pair. He kept in touch with Conrad Austin and a few other friends he had made in town and continued to deflect the advances of young eligible women that seem to crop up at every social event and there always seemed to be an upcoming ball or party on the horizon in the growing city.

In the early spring as the weather began to warm, Sam found a new distraction. He attended a baseball game at the Slag Pile Field, officially known as West End Park, located on 1st Avenue North at 6th Street adjacent to the railroad tracks. The New York Giants team was hosted by the local Birmingham Barons in an exhibition game to raise funds for the completion of the Vulcan statue to be displayed at the upcoming World's Fair. Fittingly, The Giants were led by pitcher, Joe "Iron Man" McGinnity. The game was a success as Vulcan made his appearance a week later in St. Louis, Missouri at the Louisiana Purchase Exhibition World's Fair. Sam was fascinated by the game and the large crowd it drew. There were really no stands, but crowds of people gathered around the perimeter of the makeshift field. While the players, uniforms and equipment reminded Sam of the movie, Field of Dreams, the setting for the game could not have been more different.

The field was rough, especially by 21st Century standards. Instead of cornfields, there were railroads and trains. The blue sky tried to peak through the rust colored smoke that hung over the city. But the game was enjoyed by a large crowd. Some had picnic baskets and made a day of it. As he watched the game and the crowd, Sam was reminded of his youth and watching the Barons play at the old Rickwood Field not far from where he stood now and then later playing in the new Regions Field in downtown. He missed summer nights at the ballpark with his downtown friends. He missed home.

As the heat of summer greeted the booming city, Sam encountered a familiar face while on his evening walk one night as he was greeted by Thomas Motlow while strolling down 2nd Avenue North. Young Thomas informed the Marshal that he and his brothers, Lem and Frank, better known as 'Spoon', had just opened the Motlow Brothers Distilling Company on Avenue B, and were shipping goods all over the south. It was just one of a number of new businesses that seemed to open every day to meet the needs of the burgeoning population. That same week the H.J. Porter and Company opened a new three-story store on 1st Avenue. It was perhaps the first of the large-scale department stores that would anchor the downtown business district for the next seventy years.

Sam and James continued to meet every Wednesday night. Sam always brought his friend a meal from Paul's Café and lamented the fact that they could not enjoy the meal in the restaurant. That fall, Sam did begin to have Paul prepare two plates and he would join James for their weekly meal together in his makeshift home in the blacksmith shop. Paul never inquired about the takeout or who it was for. Sam would deliver the plates back to the following morning. The excitement of the shootout and the Harland Hill mystery had waned in the months since, and the men returned to discussing events of the day and only occasionally lamented their plight and rarely mentioned hopes of returning home.

As the crisp air of autumn arrived, Sam was introduced to Dr. Laura Burton, a newly licensed medical doctor, and her husband, Dr. Allen Burton from Mobile. Irene Bullard introduced the couple at their usual Thursday evening meal and announced that Dr. Laura Burton would be joining her practice in the Watts Building and that they were looking for a bigger place to set up an infirmary. Allen would be establishing a sperate practice and the couple was in the process of looking for a residence in Birmingham. Sam was thrilled to see yet another female physician making her own way, but he sensed a tenseness between the couple although both were polite and engaging. Laura was quiet and reserved, while Allen seemed to be full of himself and loved to talk, mostly about himself.

Through the evening conversation, Sam learned that the young couple had met at medical school in Louisville and hesitated to tell them he had grown up in nearby Bardstown, since he really didn't know much about the place, but it at least made for some dinner banter. Luckily, the conversation focused more on Birmingham than Kentucky, and Sam was thankful for that.

In the coming weeks, Laura became a regular part of the group outings to theatres and dinner. Her husband rarely joined in.

As another year neared its end, Sam had exhausted all leads through official records sources but continued to look for any information he could on James's family through the various black communities throughout the city but seemed to strike out at every turn. He had to be careful because no information came easily for a white U.S. Marshal asking questions about black folks. He developed a premise that he had been contacted by an attorney for a deceased relative who was looking for a Lewis or Johnston family that had moved to the Birmingham area regarding a matter of an inheritance. Whenever he had time, he would inquire at local churches and anywhere else he thought he might get answers but after more than two years of digging, it seemed as though James's 19th Century history would indeed remain a mystery.

As Christmas came again, the city was beginning to take on a modern look with electric lights everywhere. Even though Birmingham's first telephone exchange had been established in the 1880's, phones were just recently becoming commonplace in most businesses and in a few residences. The city was transforming from the wild west movie set that Sam landed in a little over three years ago into an industrial city. The smoke and smells were ever present as were the saloons and brothels, but the city now had a assortment of theatres, fine restaurants, and hotels throughout the growing downtown area. Fine homes were being built in town and in the suburbs that in a hundred years would be considered in the heart of the city.

On his nightly walk through the city, Sam could not help but marvel at the transformation he had witnessed in the last three years, but he also longed to be home. Although his body was younger, he often still felt like the sixty-one-year-old man he would have been. As fascinating as this was at times, he longed for a hot shower and breakfast burrito and the comforts of the 21st century.

Chapter 12

1905 came in with only the cold and no snow. Sam and James continued with their routines and the city was still growing at a rapid pace.

The ornate Linn Building on the northeast corner of 1st Avenue and 20th Street North was being prepared for demolition to make way for the second skyscraper that would eventually anchor the heaviest corner on earth. The building was home to Birmingham's first bank, built in 1873. It was an ornate three-story building that had been dubbed Linn's Folly because of its extravagant appearance among the wooden framed structures that dominated the city at the time. Though the ground floor was the bank headquarters, the elaborate third story ballroom was host to the annual Calico Ball each New Year's Eve. The building was still beautiful and in sound condition, but progress called for its demise to make way for the 16-story Brown-Marx Building, that once completed, would surpass the Woodward as the tallest building in Alabama.

Vulcan had arrived back in town, disassembled and riding on a train. By most accounts the creation and display of the massive iron man and his appearance at the world's fair was a success. The statue garnered the grand prize at the event and was the envy of cities across the country. The city of St. Louis made an offer to buy the iron man and keep it in the city following the event. San Francisco wanted to purchase the statue and place it in the bay as a sort of bookend, west coast version, of the Statue of Liberty and another proposal called its placement in the Chesapeake Bay. But the leaders of Birmingham were determined that the largest cast iron man in world should come home, although no one could agree on what to do with him once he arrived.

Vulcan landed in town by mid-February and when he arrived, he sat on the train cars while the debate about what to do with him raged on. The original plan was to place the giant in the middle of the manicured capitol park but residents living in the mansions surrounding the beautiful new green space rallied against the idea of the colossal bare-ass giant staring at them every day. Residents also vetoed the idea of placing the statue in the center of the traffic circle at 5 Points South for the same reasons. Finally, a wealthy citizen and associate of steel baron, Henry Debardeleben, offered to pay off the Birmingham Commercial Clubs remaining $3,000 debt if they placed the iron man at the intersection of 20th Street and the Railroad Reservation and dedicated it in honor of Debardeleben and lighted the statue each night. Robert Jemison agreed to pay for the installation and lighting if the benefactor agreed to pay the monthly electric bill. DeBardeleben declined the honor of having a "commercial" statue named in his honor and suggested the club just scrap the iron man and donate the funds to the new Hillman Hospital. Meanwhile, the L & N Railroad that had donated the return transportation of the giant grew tired of the indecision that had left Vulcan lying on train cars just west of the station for weeks. When the company's patience was finally exhausted, they hauled the pieces to an unused sidetrack along Red Mountain and unceremoniously dumped the icon in the weeds along the side of the track.

As Spring arrived and the air warmed, Sam had all but resolved that he would live out his life in this time. If the door he went through under the viaduct was the key, he knew it would be at least another decade before the viaduct's completion. He and James continued their weekly meal and conversation every Wednesday, but any mention of 'going home' was long past. It had become to painful to consider and hope had faded as they struggled with life as it was now.

On April 26, there was a large gathering of what was surely the last of the Civil War Veteran's at a reunion downtown. A parade with more than 1,000 participants marched through the heart of the city to Capital Park for the dedication of the Confederate Soldier and Sailor Memorial. The 52-foot-tall obelisk had recently been placed at the south entrance to the park where it stood until 2020.

On one of Sam's first walks through the city he was amazed to see the obelisk wasn't there. He wasn't sure when it had been placed but remembered the night the building tension from an angry group tried to bring it down and was finally stopped with a promise from the mayor that the city would promptly remove it safely which they did 24 hours later. The monument, like similar ones across the south, had been the target for several groups as a symbol to honor racism and the Jim Crow era rather than the purpose claimed by those that supported the remembrance of so-called Southern Heritage. When Sam first visited the park, the base was in place and held an old artillery gun from the Spanish-American War that sat on top. The gun was now replaced by the by the new monument.

Today he stood at the edge of the park as speeches were made in front of the new monument and he remembered the outpouring of indignation following the murder of George Floyd by a Minneapolis Police Officer in 2020 that was the final straw in years of racial tension that had been building and finally led to the removal of this and other statues and monuments across the nation that honored civil war veterans of the Confederacy or slavery.

There was not a dark face in the large crowd that was gathered, and Sam wondered if they could ever understand how that monument was viewed by people of color or would be viewed by future generations and by history itself. As they gathered to remember and honor the veterans of the war of lost causes, he knew that not a single soul among them considered themselves as a terrorist or anything other than a patriotic citizen even though they had waged war on their own country. It was a strange time and made him more homesick for 2022.

The next parade came two weeks later when the Buffalo Bill Wild West Show came to town for a week of shows that packed Smith Park on the western edge of downtown for the extravaganza that was part rodeo and part circus. Sam avoided that one altogether.

New buildings were still appearing throughout downtown in addition to the Brown-Marx Building that was now beginning to rise. Blach's opened a new 3-story store on 3rd Avenue and the new Florence Hotel opened on the northwest corner of 2nd Avenue and 19th Street

North. The hotel had stood for more than a decade, but a new owner completely refurbished the hotel adding electric lights, an elevator, and new décor.

The city's streetcars had been updated from being drawn by mules to electric cars tethered to overhead wires that stretched throughout downtown and even out into surrounding suburbs and workplaces.

Sam was glad that the city was progressing and even more happy that the fighting and shootouts in downtown saloons were becoming much less commonplace. He had not had to draw his gun since the night he faced the Harland sons and hoped he would never have to pull it again. The paperwork load in the office had increased along with the growing population of the district. The volume had more than doubled since his arrival, but Charles was handling it without complaints. The deputies to the north were also content and Sam tried to meet with them in person twice each year. Unlike in modern times, there was no governance from D.C., so Sam handled the duties and rarely heard from anyone there. But in late September he received a letter with a familiar return address - 1600 Pennsylvania Avenue. Unlike the letter from the President, he found upon his arrival in the office on that first morning, this was a simple and succinct note but still penned in the President's own hand.

Dear Marshal Robbins,

You will learn soon of a planned trip to visit your fair city on October 25. Our train should arrive in the afternoon. We will only be there for a few hours, but I look forward to finally meeting you.

Sincerely, Theodore Roosevelt

Later that afternoon, Charles came into Sam's office with a beaming grin as he handed Sam the telegram he had just received announcing the planned arrival of the President on October 25th. The next morning, Sam was asked to attend a meeting in the mayor's office the following day to plan for the Presidential visit.

Sam slipped into the crowded office just before the 10 a.m. start time and listened to the mayor ramble on for more than an hour as the city prepared for the visit.

Among the various city workers were other city leaders, and Sam had no idea why he was invited until the newly elected mayor informed Police Chief, William Weir, that the president had personally requested that the security for his visit be handled by U.S. Marshal Sam Robbins and all heads in the room turned to stare at the Marshal leaning against the back wall. Sam was more surprised than anyone in the room but tried not to show it. The mayor asked that the Chief and Marshal meet to decide the best plan of action once the committee had ironed out all the details of the visit.

Over the next two weeks and numerous meetings Sam learned that the President would arrive in Birmingham by train at 2 PM after stops in Tuskegee and Montgomery and would depart at 7 PM on the same train headed to Memphis. There would a welcoming speech by the mayor at Union Station upon the President's arrival followed by a parade through the city to Capital Park, where a platform was being built in front of the Confederate Monument for the President's address.

Roosevelt was the first President to have an official Secret Service detail, but it was not the kind of detail Sam was used to in the 21st century where advance teams of dozens of agents would have been in town weeks before the visit scouting every detail of his travel and stay, vetting every venue and person that would have the slightest contact or access to the President or anything he contacted.

On Monday morning, Sam learned that the President would be accompanied by two agents. Upon arrival at the train station one agent would proceed to the park with a city police officer while the other agent and Sam would accompany the President on his carriage ride through the city.

On Wednesday, October 25th, the sun was bright, and the autumn air was crisp. It was a perfect day for a Presidential visit. Just after 10 AM the telegram arrived announcing that due to a delay, the President would now be departing Montgomery at 2 PM and would arrive at Union Station in Birmingham just before 5 PM.

Sam met with Captain Andrew Marin of the Birmingham Police Department for lunch at Paul's Café. He had requested Marin be the liaison with the Secret Service as he trusted Marin's judgement to be vigilant without being overzealous. After a nice lunch the pair walked over to the south end of Capital Park where a crowd was already gathering. They then walk the route back to the train station noting any problem areas. Marin and Chief Weir had a full force of men already stationed along the route. With the new arrival time of 5 PM, they agreed to reconvene at the train station at 4 PM.

Sam walked back across the street to the hotel and got a shave in the barber shop and changed his clothes. He wanted to be at his best when meeting the President. He had seen several presidents through his years as a cop and Deputy Marshal but always from a distance and he had definitely never had one write him letters.

When the train pulled into the station at three minutes before five a large crowd had gathered at the platform. Mayor Ward and other politicians and dignitaries awaited while the police kept the crowd behind a large rope stretched along the platform. When the train came to a full stop, Sam and Andrew Marin boarded the train following the instructions they received yesterday. Once on board they were greeted by a man with a drooping mustache and bushy sideburns that matched it. He introduced himself as the President's assistant and then introduced the pair to the Secret Service agent standing at the end of the car. Agent George Doyle was a man of average height and build with steely green eyes. His mustache was less dramatic and matched his auburn hair. Both men were pleasant but seemed to be all business. After the introductions, Doyle asked the locals if they understood the plan before departing to head to the speech platform accompanied by Officer Ted Wharton, whom Marin had hand-picked for the assignment.

"I thought there were two agents," Sam asked Doyle as the three stood and waited.

"Yes. James is in with the President. He is with him at all times that we are in public," he explained. *Ah, the body man*, Sam thought.

When he worked Presidential details in the 21st century, the Secret Service always had a body man that stayed within an armlength of the President at all times. Other agents surrounded him, the number and area dependent on the

124

situation but there was always a body man and in tight quarters there may three or four.

The door at the end of the train car opened and out stepped President Theodore Roosevelt. Sam recognized the man from history books, but he looked different in person and reached out to shake both men's hand. As awestruck as Sam was with his face to face with the President, he almost lost it when he was introduced to the second Secret Service agent, James Amos. He stood about six feet tall with a slender but muscular build, his black hair was closely shorn and his face cleanly shaved... and he was an African American. The man with caramel colored skin shook both men's hands and Sam could see that Marin was as surprised as he was. Sam had been immersed in a society where men of color held only menial jobs and would certainly never be allowed to mingle with white men of prominence; yet here was a black man entrusted with the safety of the most powerful man in the United States.

"I wish we had more time, Marshal but it is certainly a pleasure to finally meet you," Roosevelt said as they made their way to the train door. Amos handed the President his hat as he stepped off the train to a roar of the crowd. James Amos placed his own bowler hat on his head and walked about two steps behind the President. Sam and Marin followed.

The President was introduced to Mayor George Ward and the crowd by Alabama Great Southern Railway President Frank Y. Anderson who had provided the train for the Presidential tour of the south. Mayor Ward, who had planned a short speech seemed overwhelmed by the moment and instead had the look of a frightened deer before stammering that he had forgotten what he was going to say before finally spurting out, "Welcome to our fine city, Mr. President!"

After a hearty handshake with the mayor, Roosevelt smiled and said, "Mr. Mayor, that's the finest speech I've heard since I left Washington!"

The men stepped from the platform into the waiting carriage. James took a seat next to the driver with the President and mayor in the rear seat. Sam and Marin stood on the board affixed to the rear as the carriage pulled away from the platform turning north on 20th Street. The carriage was preceded by a marching band, followed by an honor guard of Civil War Veterans on horseback. The streets were lined with people cheering as the carriage approached and after it had passed. The President waving to the crowds that seemed eager to see him. Sam and Marin constantly scanned the crowds, as did James Amos in the front. Two Police officers on horseback escorted the carriage and two more followed behind. At least two officers manned each intersection as the parade passed.

There was a slight chill in the air, but the sun had shone brightly all day and was now glowing in the western horizon making it a perfect backdrop for a Presidential convoy and speech. As the carriage cleared the intersection of 5th Avenue Sam saw a heavy bearded man step to the front of the crowd with a pistol in his left hand. Sam instantly leapt from the carriage and tackled the man into the crowd. The gun skittered along the curb and with the man pinned to the sidewalk, Sam looked up to see Marin and four other officers looming over him as the carriage continued down the street. Sam sprang to his feet and instructed the officers to take the man to the jail. Marin handed them the pistol he'd recovered and the pair ran to catch the carriage. Sam wasn't sure if the President had even noticed the commotion but as they hopped back aboard, James Amos turned and tipped his hat at the pair with a nod that indicated a job well done.

As they neared the platform at the park Sam could see that it was now illuminated in lights as the sky dimmed. The President was introduced to the crowd by Rufus Rhodes, the publisher of the Birmingham News. Sam and Marin took their positions at either end of the platform and tried to remain inconspicuous. James Amos stood behind the platform about eight feet directly behind the President and invisible to the crowd. Sam could not help but note that stoic African American man was standing on the base of the Confederate monument. It was an ironic image.

Roosevelt's speech was very Presidential as he spoke of the industrial development and progress in Alabama and said that the city's rise was not only due to the abundance of natural resources, but also the quality of the people. He noted that he was greeted at the train station and led here by an Honor Guard of Civil War veterans from both sides of the conflict. "The men who wore blue and the men who wore gray, united forever!" He said as the crowd cheered.

Following the speech, the President and a small entourage of dignitaries boarded one of the new electric streetcars and headed west to the Alabama State Fairgrounds where another crowd awaited his arrival. After another brief speech, the President headed back to town and boarded his special train to Memphis. It was now almost 7:30

127

in the evening and the President said his farewells aboard the streetcar and once they arrived at the train station, he, Doyle, and Amos boarded the train that seconds later pulled away from the platform.

Sam thanked Marin and Chief Wier and commended them on the fine job the department had done remarking that he wasn't sure the President was even aware of the man with the gun. Weir said that his officers reported that the man was "shitfaced drunk" and totally unaware of what was going on, but he was booked in on charges of drunkenness and brandishing a deadly weapon.

Sam was hungry but supper would have to wait. He couldn't wait to tell James about the day and most of all about James Amos, so he headed straight up Morris to the shop. As he approached, James was just closing the large doors out front, and Sam gave him a tip of the hat before placing his finger on the side of his nose and kept walking. He slipped around to the back in the darkness of the night where James stood waiting at the rear door.

Sam was like a giddy schoolboy telling James all about meeting the President and about meeting James Amos. After a twenty-minute recap of the day, Sam apologized for his excitement and told James he had not forgotten their meal. He slipped out the back again and headed to pick up their usual Wednesday night meal at Paul's. When he returned both men ate and talked. The excitement of a Presidential visit and seeing a black man in a position of importance seemed to fuel new energy in them both.

Chapter 13

James and Sam had a Christmas meal together again in the quiet of the room at the blacksmith shop with no celebration really. No mention was made of home but both men longed to be back in their own time but had abandoned all hope by this point.

The winter months of 1906 were fairly mild and uneventful as the city continued to grow both in population with buildings under construction everywhere. Mine explosions and cave-ins were not uncommon but rarely did more than slow production for a day or two and since the mines were on the outskirts of the city, most people were only aware of the disasters when they read of them in the newspapers.

With no Presidential visits or other historic events on the horizon, Sam settled back into his daily routine. James did too, working in the blacksmith shop that continued to stay busy despite the growing influx of automobiles in the city. Many of the warehouses along Morris Avenue were now lined with delivery trucks instead of horses and wagons.

In March the Board of Aldermen voted to place the Vulcan statue in the center of Capitol Park as originally planned, but the uproar of citizens in the neighborhood grew louder and no action was taken to implement the installation as Vulcan continued lying in pieces in weeds along the railroad tracks on the side of Red Mountain.

Sam had continued spending time with Dr. Irene Bullard, Dr. Laura Burton, and Dr. Thaxton at least twice a month for dinner or more frequently if there was a new show in town. The group was quite comfortable together, but Sam often wondered where Laura's husband was as he was never mentioned. In mid-March Thaxton caught up with Sam as he walked away from the restaurant after the group had said their goodbyes. He told Sam that he was concerned about Laura. He explained that the couple had been separated since shortly after their arrival in town and she had been granted a divorce just last week. He explained that her husband's medical practice had failed and that he had been unable to obtain a job and continually showed up their offices and the two had heated arguments and that he feared for Laura's safety.

The next morning Sam went by their offices in the Watts Building on 3rd Avenue on his morning walk. He saw Laura at her desk and spoke to her discreetly, but she assured him that all was good. She explained that last month she had agreed to remarry Allen and they had set a wedding date of May 9th. She explained that her husband could be hard to deal with especially after his practice failed but he was now reestablishing his medical practice and they were going to try and repair their marriage. She thanked Sam for his concern but assured him all was well.

A week later, on April 8th, Irene called Sam to ask his advice. It seems that Allen's practice had failed again before it ever got started and Laura had called off the wedding. This seemed to infuriate the spurned husband who showed up at their offices that evening and at the new infirmary the following morning begging Laura to take him back and being otherwise disruptive to the practice and their patients. Sam wasn't sure what to do since the laws of harassment and stalking were very different now than in his time as a cop. He sought the help of Andrew Marin who said that not much could be done unless the man made specific threats unless the doctor's swore out a warrant for his unruly conduct disrupting their business. Sam lamented that 120 years later, not much had changed and domestic harassment was still a major issue facing families and law enforcement alike.

Sam called Irene and promised that the police were aware and would keep an eye on both Laura and the practice. He also spoke to Laura, but she seemed embarrassed and assured him that it would all blow over. Sam told both women to call the police if Allen showed up again.

When Sam arrived back at his at his office after lunch on April 10th, he knew something was awry when he found Captain Andrew Marin and Sergeant Ted Wharton waiting in his office. They came to break the news in person and to ask for assistance.

It seems that yesterday evening, Allen Burton had shown up at Laura's home very angry and demanding to speak to her. Not wanting another confrontation, she slipped out the back and took refuge at the next-door neighbor's house watching out the window for him to leave. She had left Dr. Thaxton who was at her house along with another friend, Mrs. V.S Andrews who was recovering from surgery and Laura had offered her home as a place to recover. Thaxton and Mrs. Andrews assured the ex-husband that Laura had not returned home from the office, but he insisted on waiting and so the pair made small talk while the angry man paced and waited.

After more than twenty minutes, Laura decided he was not leaving, and she would have to confront him. She borrowed a cloak and scarf to maintain the pretense that she was just returning home and to not further escalate his anger. Mrs. Andrews had reported that once Laura returned an argument ensued and the divorced couple left the room and could be heard arguing loudly in the adjacent room. After several minutes Laura emerged back into the sitting room with Mrs. Andrews and Dr. Thaxton followed by Allen Burton who continued to try to convince Laura that they needed to talk this out and that walking away was not the answer. He insisted that they go back in private to continue their discussion, but Laura refused and asked him again to leave the house. Instead, Allen retreated to the room alone and emerged with a 32-caliber Smith and Wesson revolver in hand. Seeing the gun, Mrs. Andrews fled out the front while Dr. Thaxton intervened pleading for calm. Burton fired twice into Thaxton at close range and then fired at his wife as she reached the door, striking her in the breast. As she stumbled away from the house, Allen caught up to her, firing again shooting her in the neck at close range. He then dropped the gun and pulled a pocketknife from his pocket and slit his own throat, his body falling beside his dead ex-wife on the front lawn. Neighbors responded to the carnage and tended to Thaxton and called police. Dr. Thaxton was transferred to Hillman Hospital but had not regained consciousness.

Sam was devastated by the news and knew then what assistance the pair of officers had come to request. Someone had to tell Irene. When he arrived at her office she was in tears and had already heard the news. He sat in silence with her for the next two hours. Words would never be adequate. He knew the feeling of loss all too well. He called some of her friends to stay with her through the night before going to check on his friend Dr. Thaxton. He arrived at Hillman Hospital only minutes after the dentist was pronounced dead. He was told by the doctors there that the two bullets had penetrated his intestines and infection had set in quickly. Sam left even more devastated. He knew that a similar wound in 2022 would not have been pleasant, but that with modern surgical techniques and antibiotics the patient would likely recover. Sam felt trapped in this God-forsaken time and had lost two friends to a senseless act that could have come from the headlines of the local TV news in 2022.

It was only Monday, but Sam couldn't wait until Wednesday. He needed to talk this out with James and after supper, he made his way to the back of the blacksmith shop and waited in the shadows until some railroad men finished whatever they were doing on the train, and it slowly chugged away. He knocked softly on the back door and a moment later James opened the door and immediately recognized the distress in his friend's eyes.

Sam relayed the entire scenario to his friend who patiently listened and consoled him in his grief. That grief was certainly compounded by their presence here. Both men felt trapped but rarely talked about it anymore. There was no use. Nothing was going to change. Before the night was over, they both realized that their silence on the matter was not helping anything either. All they had was each other. While talking wasn't going to get either one of them home, it just might keep them from losing their minds here. They agreed to talk more often and then sat in silence for the next two hours with the comfort of each other's presence.

Chapter 14

The summer of 1906 was hot and uneventful. The afternoons of late summer made Sam long for air conditioning and James was surprised to learn that in 2022 air-conditioners were commonplace, even in modest homes.

Sam got some refreshment from his daily indulgence of Coca-Cola, which was now served everywhere it seemed. He also was seeing advertisements for a new drink popping up in town. Buffalo Rock Ginger Ale was being distributed by the Alabama Grocery Company located on 1st Avenue North. While the grocery wholesaler distributed a number of products under the 'Alabama" label, its president, Sidney Lee, had been working for the last three years with a chemist from Selma named Ashby Coleman to create a carbonated drink from the ginger-based tonic the grocer sold. The drink finally made its debut as Buffalo Rock and was an instant hit with customers. Sam remembered the curiously strong drink that his mother loved and insisted on him drinking whenever he had a stomachache as a kid. In 2022 it was also staple ingredient in many of the hip bars in town that had built cocktails on the ginger ale that was uniquely Birmingham.

Sam and James continued their weekly Wednesday night meals and now talked more openly about their feelings trying to support each other without turning things into an all-out pity party. Sam confessed again that he had a tinge of guilt because he knew his plight was so much better than James's. James laughed and told him that his tales of the future were often all that kept him going. They each continued their daily routines and looked forward to their Wednesday night meetings.

By October, Vulcan had been rescued from abandonment by a plan to display the iron giant at the Alabama State Fairgrounds for the upcoming State Fair. It was considered a temporary fix until a suitable home could be found but all agreed that it was better than the statue lying rusting in the weeds.

An elaborate plan was developed to get the icon to the Fair Grounds. He would be loaded on a train from the abandoned rail line where he was dumped more than twenty months earlier. From there the train would transport the disassembled icon to Bessemer where the cars could be switched to the streetcar line and pull the giant back to the Fair Grounds for off-loading. The streetcar line proudly announced that since Vulcan was only two years old, he qualified for a free ride. He arrived at the Fair Grounds on Sunday, October 13 and was hastily assembled for his debut to fair goers on Wednesday. In their haste to get him bolted back together his right arm was attached backwards causing the giant's arm to point upward in what appeared to be a painfully contorted twist. His spear tip had been lost and had to be recast, but it didn't matter because his upside-down hand could no longer hold it. The new spear tip was instead left at the iron man's feet.

Back in the city, the 16-story Brown-Marx Building was opened and despite the skepticism that the building was too large for the city, it was completely leased at opening. The buildings namesake's Marx and Company, an investment banking firm, and real estate company, Brown Brothers, were joined by a host of other firms staking offices in the new tower. Most were the offices of steel and mining companies. The building was financed by the Tennessee Coal Iron and Railroad Company who also held offices there. The immediate success of the building caused iron magnate William Woodward to purchase the new tower and he immediately launched plans to double the size of the skyscraper by adding a duplicate structure adjacent to it that would be connected to form one massive skyscraper.

As the Christmas holiday approached, the new city saw decorations appearing in some stores and along the downtown streets. The city was fulfilling the aspirations of Mayor George Ward who was hell bent on turning the city into a decent place to live and work. The mayor had added police to quell the violence, increased the fire department adding stations and more firemen to keep up with the growth and had also insisted on green spaces to make the city beautiful. Along with the city's centerpiece, Capital Park, the mayor also spruced up West Park located between 16th and 17th Streets and 5th and 6th Avenues, and East Park located between 24th and 25th Streets and 6th and 7th Avenues. The three parks were part of the original layout of the city and the mayor invested in a beautification plan for all three.

West Park featured a stone grotto and was surrounded by the 16th Street Baptist Church, Henley School, and Temple Emanu-El.

Christmas came and Sam joined James for their annual Christmas feast in the blacksmith shop. The pair ate well every Wednesday night, but on Thanksgiving and Christmas, they went all out, even though Thanksgiving had not yet caught on as a favored holiday in the south, both men had fond memories gathered with family and friends.

The new year saw continued growth and changes to Birmingham's government. A change that was filled with controversy. As Sam witnessed the upheaval and read the daily updates in the newspaper, he couldn't help but think that not much had changed in this regard. In the 21st century Birmingham was a tiny democratic island in a very republican state. If the city passed any ordinance that was too left leaning the state legislature would quickly pass a law to undo it. In 2016, the city council passed an ordinance raising the minimum wage in the city from $7.25 to $10.10 but before the law could be implemented, the state legislature passed a law barring municipality from setting minimum wage effectively reversing the city's ordinance.

In 1907, Mayor George Ward was re-elected by a slim margin over challenger Frank O'Brien. O'Brien, who owned and operated the local Opera House and had campaigned on a promised to beef up the undermanned police force and had campaigned fervently against the incumbent.

Ward had painted O'Brien as a puppet of the Saloon and Liquor industries. He had earned a reputation as an Alderman and Mayor for strict enforcement of saloon regulations to change the city's image which he thought was a better alternative to outright prohibition. As mayor, he had also advanced the city government organization by instituting a codified Municipal Code for the first time. He had also invested heavily in his "City Beautiful" campaign of sprucing up public parks and buying more land for future parks. He had also added police officers, firefighters and added new fire station in an ever-continuing effort to keep up with the city's fast growth.

Following his narrow re-election, the State legislature passed a new municipal code which changed the balance of power in the city government. Previously, the mayor held one vote in meetings of the Board of Aldermen and made all committee appointments. Under the new law, the city government was separated into legislative and executive branches and gave the mayor only the power of a veto over the Board, while increasing his power to hire and fire city workers. Ward had supported the legislation with the understanding that it would not take effect until the next term. However, the law became effective while the mayor was on a six-week vacation in Europe. In his absence, the Board of Aldermen voted 10-7 to reorganize the government as a City Council with John Parker as President and Acting Mayor. Parker immediately reassigned committees, leaving Ward's supporters primarily in charge of the cemetery issues.

Upon his return, Ward, with the support of Police Chief Wier, who had also been reelected, chose to ignore the Board's actions during his absence and called a meeting of the Board of Aldermen and refused to allow Council members to take seats as officers of the city. Ward's allies introduced legislation in the state to prohibit municipal reorganization before the 1908 city elections, but it failed. Parker filed suit against Ward and won a judgement in the Alabama Supreme Court giving the Council control of the city. The main purpose of the anti-Ward delegation had been to loosen the restrictions on saloons, but that was all for naught as a county-wide prohibition was passed in the general election to take effect on January 1, 1908.

Knowing that prohibition would be coming, sent a wave through the city's saloons and the sole distillery operating in the city owned and operated by the Motlow family. Some saloons prepared for shutdown while others simply moved their businesses out of the county and still others moved underground as bootleggers that would, no doubt, be in demand in the coming year.

Another legislative action that would have an even greater impact on the city came in August when Governor B. B. Comer signed the Greater Birmingham legislation laying the groundwork for a referendum allowing the several surrounding municipalities to vote on whether they wanted their city to be annexed into the City of Birmingham. If all approved, it would increase the city from 3 square miles to almost 48. The growing population would immediately swell from 45,000 to more than 133,000.

While Sam found all the controversy interesting, it really didn't affect his duties or his routines. He and James continued their Wednesday night suppers and conversations. Their discussions varied depending on the mood and events of the week but they both tried to stay positive. They had resolved that if they ever made it back to their time it would not be in their control. Neither man had expected, nor sought to experience what had happened but it did. If there was a way back, it would likely happen in a similar fashion. The thought gave them some peace but both men still longed for home.

The coming prohibition seemed to fuel even more building and investment. The addition to the new Brown-Marx building was underway to more than double the size of Alabama's tallest building. Ground preparations were underway for the city's grandest building yet, the Terminal Station. Work on an underpass leading to the new station was proceeding on 5th Avenue North. Sam never saw the beautiful building as it was demolished when he was only five years old after decades of neglect. Only the underpass remained as a constant reminder of a past time when railways were the mode of travel and of a hasty decision to not preserve the beauty of the train staion.

Sam watched as saloons closed and other businesses moved in. The most elaborate saloon to close was the Bank Restaurant and Saloon on the northwest corner of 1st and 20th. Sam knew that it would eventually be replaced by the Empire Building but he wasn't sure when it would be built. The large saloon was not all that impressive in curb appeal. A simple two-story brick building that held treasures on the inside. Sam remembered gasping the first time he walked in and saw the place. Even the entrance was impressive with large swinging doors made of hand carved oak. The floors were beautifully veined marble, and the room featured a massive copper chandelier in the center of the ornate tin tiled ceiling. Most impressive was the 32-foot-long mirror behind the mahogany bar that featured silver spigots to serve customers. The owners also had a liquor and cigar wholesale business next door, so their businesses would be devastated with coming law. Like most other large saloons, they were not waiting for the end of the year and simply closed their business and sold the building. Sam couldn't help but wonder what would happen to all the treasures it held. Many of the hip bars in his neighborhood tried to recreate nostalgia and ambience and would love to have any of those pieces that were likely headed to the scrap pile.

As summer ended and the Christmas season approached, Sam attended several balls and parties simply to appease his friends and acquaintances. It seemed that each one tried to "out-do" the last one and it appeared that high society was now a part of the city. There were new people still flocking to the city to take advantage of the growth and the industrial wealth that seemed to be everywhere.

Sam attended a large gathering of the city's elite on the Saturday before Christmas at the Hotel Hillman on 4th Avenue and 19th Street. It was the city's premiere hotel and featured a grand ballroom that was the perfect setting for such extravagant gatherings. Sam usually stood in the corner and bided his time so that he could say he made appearance before slipping out the door. Generally, when folks engaged him at such an event, they needed advice or a favor or perhaps had an eligible daughter or niece that they wanted to introduce. Otherwise, the Marshal was generally ignored.

He was caught off guard when Circuit Judge A. O. Lane approached him accompanied by a skinny young lad who looked to be maybe twenty-five years old. Sam had occasional dealings with the old judge but didn't really know him all that well.

"Marshal, I want you to meet a new lawyer who just moved into town. This is Hugo Black. He is just setting up practice here."

It was all Sam could do to keep from spitting the mouthful punch he had just sipped all over the future Supreme Court Justice. He was able to regain composure and shook the young man's hand.

"Glad to meet you, sir," was all he could muster before the pair moved on to someone else.

Sam had spent his twelve years as a Deputy Marshal in the Birmingham Federal Court Building that bore the name "Hugo L. Black United States Courthouse."

The following Wednesday was Christmas and Sam and James held their usual feast. Hugo Black was the subject of much of the conversation that night. James confessed that he admired Black and told Sam that he was first a student at the Birmingham Medical College before moving to study law at the University of Alabama Law School. But he first heard of the man when the Supreme Court voted unanimously in Brown versus Board of Education ruling that segregation was unconstitutional in public schools. He confessed that he also had a twinge of mistrust for the man when he later learned of his affiliation in his early days with Klan.

Sam told him that he had read several books on the man and felt that his actions in his later life provided plenty of evidence that he did truly change. In 1965, Black joined other justices in another unanimous decision reversing the acquittal of 18 Klansmen in Mississippi for murdering three civil rights workers. Although

143

only half the Klansmen ended up being convicted, his civil rights record was stellar as a justice.

James teased Sam that he was getting to meet all these famous historical figures and that if they ever did make it back home that he would probably find out his face was now on the twenty-dollar bill or something. Sam laughed and made a reference to being the 1900 version of Forrest Gump, which then led to a lengthy explanation of the fictional character and his exploits.

Sam had now been here more than six years and James had been here for eight. They were settled, but certainly not content. Both men had long ago decided to just try and survive. Both men harbored a deep hope that one day this would end, and they would awaken in their own time, but with each passing year that seemed more and more unlikely.

Chapter 15

As 1909 arrived the city seemed transformed by prohibition. There was plenty of debauchery still going on and the police stayed busy now chasing down bootleg operations. The brothels seemed to flourish and some of those bootleggers found the houses a good outlet for their merchandise. Overall, those houses were congregated in certain red-light areas of town, and though they were technically illegal, they were rarely bothered if they did not create a reason to draw the attention of the police.

Sam and James continued their respective routines and their weekly meal. James was spending more time out of the shop as the blacksmith business was changing with more and more automobiles being used. The shop had increased its repair business on wagons and carriages and James traveled all over the city delivering the wagons following repairs. The majority of his time was still spent over the hot anvil but getting out for a few hours each week was a pleasant change.

The politics were somewhat calmer but with city elections held every two years it seemed that it was always campaign season. Sam was glad that TV had not yet been invented, otherwise the airwaves would be constant political ads as they are in election years in the 21st Century. Mayor Ward had confided in Sam that he would not seek reelection in order to run for the position of Jefferson County Sheriff in 1910.

Building continued at a rapid pace. The third anchor of the heaviest corner was completed with the Empire Building. It surpassed the Brown-Marx Building which was being transformed into an H-Shaped bemouth more than twice its original size. Plans were now underway for the fourth and final building at the intersection. The bank building would be the tallest yet. All over town the buildings seemed to get taller and more ornate. Two blocks north of the heaviest corner, the Farley Building on the corner of 3rd Avenue and 20th Street opened, and one block west down 1st Avenue the Lincoln Life Building opened housing the Chamber of Commerce. All were examples of architecture and extravagance of the era and buildings that would endure the change of the coming decades and last well into the next century. Last, but certainly not least, the grand Terminal Station was nearing completion at 5th Avenue and 26th Street.

The grandest passenger train station in the south held its grand opening on April 6, welcoming crowds that came to marvel at the massive building and the passengers that used it to travel near and far.

Summer came and Frank O'Brien was sworn in as the new Mayor of Birmingham, having run unopposed. Sam knew the new Mayor from his time as Sherriff and as the owner of the Opera House. He was a decent man, but he was a politician. Sam offered congratulations. Weir was reelected as Chief of Police and Sam had developed a good working relationship with him.

As the skyscrapers rose all around the city, the streets were filled with shoppers and businesses. The warehouses along 1st Avenue and

Morris were busier than ever and the railroads and steel plants were too. As industries grew, the smells and haze they emitted also increased. It seemed worse in the summer as the smoke seemed to hover in the valley. At its worst, the tops of some of the tallest buildings were obscured by it. Sam had vague memories of the city in late 1960s, when the downtown was often shrouded in a deep Tang-colored fog, before the EPA took steps to curb pollution. He wasn't sure if that was what cleared things up or if it was simply that the industries were fewer, dying off as steel became cheaper to import. By the time he was a teenager the skies had cleared but much of the damage it caused still remained.

Today was a rough day. Although it was only mid-May, the heat had already arrived, and the humidity was heavy. Sam never thought he would miss TV Meteorologists, but he did. The people on the streets seemed unfazed by the heavy conditions as he went for his morning walk. As he made his way down 1st Avenue, he saw James emerge from 24th Street and turn right on 1st. He was driving a carriage that looked almost brand new. Although cars were becoming more commonplace, carriages and wagons were still the predominate mode of travel for those wealthy enough to afford it. Most in the city relied on the streetcars to get them where they needed to be.

James was delivering the carriage to a family in East Lake. Once outside the city center and past Sloss-Sheffield Steel and Iron Company, the air began to clear. It still looked as though it may rain, so James wanted to get his delivery made before having to deal with it. Once the carriage was delivered and the owner satisfied

147

with the work, James would take the dummy line back from East Lake to the stop on 2nd Avenue. The delivery was uneventful, and the customer was pleased with his carriage. As James began his walk to catch the streetcar, he heard screams coming from the lake pavilion and saw someone thrashing in the water and another grasping an overturned canoe. Several bystanders on the dock and lake's edge screamed and were highly agitated, but no one seemed to be taking any action to help.

At that moment, the James Lewis of 1909 succumbed to the 21st Century doctor as he sprinted to the lake and dove in. By the time he reached the boat only an elderly woman clinging to the canoe was visible. She was crying and saying something about her grandbaby as James went under. The murky water was dark, and he felt around hoping to find something, but he felt nothing as his lungs began to burn. As his head cleared the surface, he saw the old lady still holding on as he filled his lungs and dove again. He dove twice more desperately trying to feel or see anything in the murky green depths and then he felt it. He could see a shadowy figure as his lungs ached. He put his arm around the child and headed for the glimmering light above. The body was limp. As they broke the surface and he gasped in the fresh air he thought he heard the old lady shout, but he was now in survival mode and could think of nothing but making it to the grassy bank that was twenty yards away. He swam toward the shore with the lifeless body just above the surface. He reached the grassy bank and could see the body he carried was that of a little girl, maybe ten years old, her pale skin now a bluish purple as he felt for a pulse. There was none. He straddled the little girl lying on the grass and cleared her airway as he started chest compressions. His medical training had put the exhausted doctor into auto-pilot mode. CPR training was introduced as a new concept during his second year of med school, and this was the first time he had performed the technique on a patient. After several compressions there was still no response and he administered mouth to mouth with five quick breaths and resumed chest compressions. As he thrust down the second time on the small chest, he was hit with a face full of the murky water expelled from the little girl and he stopped. He rolled her over on her side and gave her a rap between the shoulder blades and more water came. Then she opened her eyes but was out of it. James then noticed that he was now surrounded by people staring down at them as he tried to catch his own breath.

"Is there a doctor nearby?" he finally gasped. The stunned crowd was silent. Then James remembered the old lady and looked back at the lake to see two young men hoisting her into a canoe.

"Doc Barrett lives right over yonder," a teenage girl said pointing to a house across the street.

"Is he home?" James asked as he scooped up the little girl in his arms. Her skin color was back to somewhat normal, but she was cold and having trouble maintaining consciousness. He didn't wait for an answer and ran toward the house. As he approached the front, an old man came out. He was bald with dark, deep-set eyes and a drooping mustache.

"Are you the doctor?" James asked "I pulled her from the lake and performed CPR. She expelled a lot of water, and her color has returned but her pulse is thready. I am afraid she is going into shock," James blurted without taking a breath. He then saw the astonished look on the doctor's face looking at the little girl and then at the muscular black man holding her and barking nonsense at him.

"Bring her in," he said and started back up the steps and into the house. "Lay her there," he said pointing to a large sofa. He came back with a black leather bag and began to check the child. A lady appeared and said that the ambulance was on its way. The child then began to respond to the doctor's questions and seemed to be regaining her senses. Soon, the doctor turned his attention back to James who sat in the floor beside the sofa, wet and exhausted. From the look on the doctor's face, he knew he was going to have some explaining to do.

"Now, what was all this stuff you were telling me you did?"

"I dove in and found her. When I pulled her out, I laid her on the ground and she threw up a lot of water and someone in the crowd told me you were a doctor, so I brought her right over," James answered hoping the CPR and pulse reference had gone unnoticed in the fray.

"Well, you saved her life," he answered matter of factly. "What's your name, boy?"

James didn't like the skeptical look on the old man's face nor the tone of the question and suddenly remembered he had not been in character using his 1900 accent, but it was too late for that now.

"I am James Lewis, sir. I work for Mr. James Horton, the blacksmith on Morris Avenue. I just delivered a carriage over to Mr. Ferguson and was headed back to the dummy line when I saw the boat and all."

The doctor still appeared perplexed. "Well, you better git on back then," he said looking at the door and James knew his welcome was over. He headed for the streetcar.

As he passed the pavilion, the crowd had dispersed but several people were milling about, and he saw a small group of men talking to the two boys that had rescued the old lady and overheard just enough to quicken his pace.

"I tell you it wuz a nigger man! He pulled her outa the water and then he kissed her right on the mouth and she threw up a bunch of water..."

James knew better than to hang around and was thankful the car was ready to pull away as he jumped on the back and headed back to town. The fact that he had saved the young girl's life didn't matter. If he could be identified, he would be hanging from a tree by sundown. The fear fueled a renewed energy after the exhaustion, and he wasn't sure what to do other than keep his head down and hope that no one in the car noticed his wet overalls. He got back to the shop, and no one seemed to notice his appearance as he was almost dry again. He went back to work but kept an eye out hoping for Sam to pass by so he could signal him that he needed to talk. It was only Monday, so he couldn't wait two more days for their regular meeting time. Sam would be able to find out how the girl and old lady were and whether or not the rumors of him were growing or fading. He knew the answer to that already but held out hope that

151

his saving the young girl's life might placate the fact that a black man had not only touched a white girl but had actually put his mouth on hers. He was sure that the retelling of that image would only grow with each recitation.

Later that afternoon, James saw the familiar lanky shadow across Morris walking west. He went to the door as if he were checking from something and then turned to meet Sam's glance for a fleeting moment and rubbed the side of his nose with his finger before heading back in. Sam kept walking.

As the shadows dropped across the city and the sun faded, the smog that had enveloped downtown all day was finally lifting. Sam left his office and made straight for the blacksmith shop before supper. He knew that if James needed him enough to signal, that it was important and couldn't wait. As he approached the shop, James was closing the doors, so Sam went around back. He waited in the shadows for three men to finish unloading lumber from a train car onto a wagon and then slipped to the back door where James was waiting.

"Hey man, are you okay?" he asked reading the concern on James's face.

"I am for now, but it has been a helluva day," he answered closing the door behind them.

James related the events of the morning as Sam sat mesmerized by it all and could hear both the compassion and fear in his friend's voice.

"The doc is Dr. Nathaniel Barrett. He is not only the local doc, but he is the mayor of East Lake. Has been since they incorporated in 1900. He is also chummy with the local Klan and may even be a member," Sam said shaking his head. "Did you tell him about the resuscitation?"

"When I first saw him coming out of his house, I wasn't thinking, I just blurted out a condition report of the girl, you know, doctor to doctor," James said thinking back on the chaotic scene. "Once we got her in the house and I saw she was coming around, he asked me what happened and I said that I pulled her out of the water and that when I got her to the bank, she threw up water and someone told me a doctor lived in the house, so I was bringing her to him. I am not sure he was convinced but he didn't ask me anything else and then told me to leave. If he did hear me, I am sure I used the term CPR and he wouldn't have known what that was, but I did realize that I was talking in my normal voice, and that may have given him enough cause to look suspiciously at me like he did. I did tell him my name and why I was in the neighborhood, and he seemed okay with that, but I don't have a good feeling about him. Especially after I heard the conversation with the men at the pavilion... I felt that same fear that I did in 1963 right before I ended up here."

"I will go out there tomorrow and see what I can find out without causing too much more suspicion. I'll go to Hillman and see if the child is there and check on the lady with her. Let's not panic just yet but try to stay low until I find out more."

"No deliveries scheduled for tomorrow, thank goodness so I should be here in the shop all day."

"Okay. Are you sure you're okay, physically, I mean? That had to be pretty rough. I know you haven't been swimming in the last ten years."

"Yeah, I'm all right. Worst thing is I lost my hat somewhere. Probably at the bottom of that lake!" he said smiling, trying to ease the concern he could see in Sam's face.

"You get some rest. I will drop by tomorrow night to fill you in on what I find."

The two men embraced in a bear hug before Sam slipped out the back door.

Chapter 16

The next morning Sam made his way to Hillman Hospital and found that the girl had been admitted. Joellyn Marie Finch was 9 years old and was visiting her grandparents who had recently moved to East Lake. The doctor informed the Marshal that the girl was very lucky and should have a complete recovery with a few more days of rest and care. Her grandmother had also been pulled from the lake and was resting at home. Sam was then introduced to the girl's aunt, Mrs. Joan Finch and he thought he might faint at the sight of the woman who looked so much like his Joan. Luckily, everyone was so happy to have the Marshal inquiring on the young patient that no one asked why.

After a cordial visit, Sam spoke to the little girl who remembered very little of the ordeal other than a "negro man carrying me". Sam left the hospital and caught the streetcar to East Lake. As the car clanked its way east, Sam couldn't shake the image of the aunt and the uncanny resemblance, then it suddenly hit him. He remembered helping Joan as she pieced together her family tree. Her maternal grandmother was a Finch. She was named for ancestors. A great-aunt or something named Joan and her great-great grandmother, Marie. *Could that little girl be Joan's great-great grandmother?* As the streetcar rocked on Sam did the math although he only knew Joan's birthday, but the name Finch was not that common, and he knew her family had been in Birmingham... it was feasible.

At the East Lake pavilion, Sam found one of the boys who had rescued the lady from the lake. He worked at the park and was just arriving to work when he saw what had happened.

"I grabbed a canoe and started paddling out to the lady. Jimmy jumped in with me... he is a friend that was here" he explained. "We are paddling out and then we see the nigger man in the water too. He keeps coming up for air and keeps diving back under. I never seen a nigger swim! I don't swim good, that's why I took the canoe. Anyways, when we was almost to the lady, he pops up and he has this little girl and swims over the bank yonder and lays her out... she looked dead to me, all blue and all. We pull the lady in the canoe, and she is carrying on about her grandbaby... I found out later that was the girl. Anyway, as we start paddlin' back, I see the nigger and girl and then he's on top of her pushin' on her chest and then he kisses her full on the mouth and then starts the pushin' again and she vomited all over him and starts coughing and choking and he rolls her over and hits her in the back and then scoops her up and runs toward Doc Barrett's place across the street over yonder."

"Did you know this negro man?" Sam asked.

"No sir, never seen him before."

"Anybody else here yesterday say anything about knowing him?"

"Not that I heard... you lookin' to arrest him?"

"No, why would you ask that?"

"Well, he was all over that little girl... even kissed her on the mouth... I seen him do it!"

"He was saving her life!" Sam said catching himself before he went into a full rage. "Her grandmother and other family members just wanted to thank the man for saving the girl's life, that's all."

"Well, I ain't never seen him 'round here... I been working here since last summer... don't get too many niggers out here, 'cept for the maids and such."

Sam thanked the young man for his time and moved on to the see Doctor Barrett. Sam was cautious in his questioning of the old man. He was not only a doctor but also a politician with shady connections. Sam had first encountered the name as an associate of the pastor of the First Baptist Church in downtown. The men were leading a group called True Americans, a staunchly racist, anti-immigrant group that warned of the evils of those Catholics. Their membership was secret, but it didn't take Sam long to tie most of the members to the growing roster of Ku Klux Klan groups around the city.

The doctor told Sam that the man told him his name was James Lewis and that he worked for James Horton and was delivering a carriage to his neighbor, John Ferguson. He told Sam that he had confirmed the story with his neighbor and that James was indeed an employee of the blacksmith shop. To Sam's surprise the doctor was neither impressed that James had saved the young girl or with his heroic efforts in doing so.

"I do not understand why the family wants to thank the nigger," he said matter of factly. "I tell you there is something about that boy... he don't talk like a nigger and acted strangely. I found out later he was kissing the girl... that don't go over real well around here."

Sam tried to explain that the rumors of him kissing the girl were unfounded and that it seems that all he did was save the girl's life, but he could tell the doc wanted no part of it. Sam left the doctor's home and spoke to several more people in the neighborhood and the resort and soon had a sense of fear as the theme of the black man kissing a girl seemed to be the prevalent narrative from those who had any knowledge of the situation. Sam knew that nothing he could do or say would quell that.

That afternoon Sam talked to a reporter with the Birmingham News whom he had developed a friendly professional relationship and pitched the idea of publishing the story of the rescue and touting James as the hero, but his friend declined and warned that publishing such a story would have the opposite response than intended.

"All people are going to read is a negro man touched a white girl, they are not going to be bothered with the circumstances of whether he did it to save her life. Then, someone else will expand the story and find people who saw him kissing her and it will escalate from there," he warned. "Do the man a favor and let it be." Sam took his advice and decided the best plan would be to make sure James remained safe until this story had a chance to blow over.

Sam went by the shop on his way to supper and told James all he had found out that day and pleaded with him to stay at the shop and not be out alone.

"If anyone is planning to do you harm it will only happen when they have a chance to do it and there are enough of them together. I know how these assholes work. They are brave as long as the numbers and odds are heavily in their favor so just don't give them an opportunity. I cancelled my trip to Huntsville, so I can stay close by. I haven't said anything to the police because too many of them are now Klan related. The hate for immigrants and Catholics in particular is growing, and of course, you know they already hate your race."

"Yeah, I hear the talk," James said in a soft voice. "The men come in here and talk. They don't care that I am standing right there. I'm no different to them than the horses and mules. It's crazy because almost every one of them is either an immigrant themselves or their parents or grandparents were. It's really stupid."

"Hey, that shit is still prevalent in 2022, I am ashamed to say," Sam said shaking his head in disgust. "To change the subject to a better topic, Paul is cooking fried chicken tomorrow, so at least we will have a good meal."

Sam stopped at the door and pleaded again for his friend to remain vigilant and stay put as much as he could.

"You know I rarely leave here after dark, but don't worry about me. I have had to be careful my whole life and especially since I have been in this century."

The men hugged and Sam went on his way, but his worry was deep. It wasn't just James's situation; it was the growing clamor of hate in the city. It seemed the us against them mentality of 2022 had found its way back to the past. Sam had been here almost eight years now and had grown somewhat accustomed to the disregard for black people although he hated it. But the growing ill will toward Catholics, Jews, and anyone else that wasn't a white Protestant was way too familiar to Sam and he wondered why he wasn't aware of the history, or was he just so naive that he had ignored it because he didn't fit into any of the hated categories.

The following day Sam did the paperwork that was pressing and then left the office early for lunch and headed to the County Courthouse on 3rd Avenue. After concocting a somewhat lame story and excuse regarding his need, the clerk helped him search the birth records of the Finch family starting with Joellyn Marie Finch, the girl that James had rescued. She was the daughter of Obadiah and Evelyn Finch, and Sam recognized those names as definitely being in his wife's family tree that she had painstakingly researched years ago. The girl was Joan's great-great grandmother! Sam no longer doubted this fact. As he left the courthouse, he could not help but think that this was yet one more coincidence in this madding web of bizarre entanglements with him and James through two centuries. He was eager to get James's take it on at their meal tonight.

Throughout the day, Sam made a point of passing in front of the blacksmith shop several times to make sure James was safe. Each time, all was quiet, and he thought maybe he was more paranoid than he needed to be. He stopped in front of the hotel before going in as the last of the buildings across the street came down to make way for the new skyscraper. The Alabama Bank Building was a modest three-story structure that had stood for more than three decades. It was demolished along with the western half of the McAdory building and several smaller buildings along Morris Avenue to make way for the new American Trust and Savings Building that when complete would be the tallest building in Alabama surpassing the new Empire building and completing what would soon be referred to as the heaviest corner on earth. Sam stood and marveled at the buildings surrounding the intersection and others that he could see across the city. When he landed here eight years ago, none of the skyscrapers were here. He had truly witnessed the rise of the Magic City but longed to be home when these iconic buildings were celebrated for their more recent redevelopment as hotels, office spaces and condos. He headed up to his room for a quick nap before meeting James for their weekly meal. He had so much to tell him.

Sam awoke from his nap and saw the glow of the streetlamps down Morris from his window and jumped to his feet fearing he had overslept. He looked at his watch, it was only five past six. He had only slept for an hour but had finally gotten some good rest. He hadn't slept well since James's brush with heroism and threats of lynching. He had not heard any more rumblings from the Klan or anyone else and so he may have very well blown the whole thing out of proportion, but he still had an uneasy feeling about the situation. He splashed some water on his face in the bathroom and grabbed the new hat he bought for James at Bon Ton's earlier in the day. He went by Paul's and picked up the food. It smelled so good as he made his way the blacksmith shop. He slipped around to the back and knocked on the door, but no answer came. He waited and knocked again. Still nothing. He tried not to panic. He sat the bag of food at the door along with the hat and went around front and knocked on the door but still no answer. The door was latched so he went to the back and tried the door again. It was also secured. He checked to make sure he was alone before sliding the latch open with his knife and slipping in. The place was deserted except for the horses and one mule in the stalls. James's room was empty but seemed otherwise undisturbed. Maybe he had a late delivery, but Sam was still uneasy thinking of that but there was little he could do tonight. He took the food and hat back to his hotel room and ate in solitude staring out the window at the blacksmith shop down the street.

The next morning, Sam headed for the blacksmith shop just after sunrise. The doors were opened as he approached, he decided to just go in and make any excuse for doing so. He had to make sure James was okay. He found the Horton sons working on a carriage but didn't see James. The two men were surprised to see the Marshal standing there staring.

"Uh... I am looking for the colored man that works here," he said.

"James ain't here," Robert said and went back to his work.

"Do you know when he'll be back? I need to speak to him."

"About what?" Jacob asked dropping his tool and staring at Sam with his hands on his hips.

Sam's mind was racing for a cover story, but nothing seemed plausible.

"Seems he rescued a little girl from drowning out at East Lake on Monday and the family wanted to thank him," Sam finally said.

"We don't know where he is. He stays in the back yonder but wasn't here when we got here this morning," Robert said. "That ain't like him."

"He took a wagon out to East Lake yesterday evenin' and was gonna catch the car back to town," Jacob added.

Sam's stomach twisted into a tight knot with that news. "Tell him I need to see him when he comes back," Sam said as he turned and walked away. He fought the urge to run to the streetcar line on 2nd Avenue but got there quickly enough and caught the dummy line to East Lake. He spent the next four hours asking if anyone had seen James. He confirmed with the owner that the wagon had been delivered by James at about 6:30 and that James was last seen walking north toward the streetcar stop. No one at the resort had seen him so Sam headed back to the streetcar stop and looked around for any evidence of foul play or a struggle while he waited on the streetcar to arrive. He tried not to think the worst, but his mind was flooded with scenarios that were all bad.

He boarded the streetcar and got the name of the driver on duty yesterday. The driver said that he would be back on duty tonight at five. Sam sat on the ride back into town and tried to push the bad scenes from his mind. He tried to relax, but he couldn't. He got off the car and walked back to the shop. Still no James. Sam informed Jacob that the wagon had been delivered but that no one had seen James since. Sam decided to skip lunch, his

163

stomach was still in a knot. He went back to the office but just sat at his desk. He had a really bad feeling, and he just couldn't shake it until he saw James was safe.

Sam was waiting at the 2nd Avenue stop at five. The driver remembered seeing James but said he never got on the streetcar. He said five or six men were harassing him at the stop in East Lake and he said James took off running toward the park as he was pulling away.

"They were chasing him but unless something happened, they weren't going to catch him. He was fast!" the driver explained.

Sam found some solace in the fact that James probably got away, but his fear was now confirmed that James was in trouble. Darkness and in an unfamiliar setting chased by racists. And now he'd been missing for almost twenty-four hours. Sam hopped off at East Lake and the driver pointed, confirming his last sighting of James. Sam followed the boardwalk toward the dance pavilion. He asked numerous people including workers at the roller coaster and Ferris wheel, but no one had seen a black man. He asked several people at the theatre, but still had no luck with even a sighting of James.

Sam walked around the entire property that was lighted but decided he would need to return in the light of day to explore the surrounding land. The moon was fairly bright, and he could see the charred remains of the hotel that had burned to the ground more than a decade ago. The property was surrounded by woods that provided plenty of opportunity for James to hide... or to hide a body. He tried not to go there but having been a cop all his life skewed his thinking toward the worst circumstances.

Sam caught the last train back to the city just before 10 PM. He walked back by the shop on his way to his hotel. It was dark, but he had to slip around back and knock on the door. There was still no answer.

Chapter 17

Sam didn't sleep at all and was at the streetcar as soon as there was light. He headed back to the resort and walked the property. It was quiet and desolate at this time of day. He left the resort and crossed the remains of the burned hotel foundation that was covered now in tall grass around the edges. The forest surrounding the park was thick with vegetation in the middle of the summer. Sam looked for any evidence of disturbance in the underbrush that might indicate anyone had been through but could find nothing. He headed back to the resort and saw activity around the theatre. They appeared to be setting up a new show. The John L. White's Great Alabama Minstrels was a black troupe and were the first African Americans to perform in the Birmingham area. They had just arrived, and so were of no help in locating James.

Dejected, Sam boarded the streetcar and headed back to town. He spent the next three weeks looking for James and trying to get any information he could but got nowhere. He had stopped entertaining questions as to why he was investigating a missing colored man, and just pushed on with no results. He had confirmed rumors of the white men chasing James that night, but of course, no one had come forward with a first-hand account and certainly no one had confessed to chasing him.

Sam got his work done, but now every spare moment was spent seeking answers about James but now more than a month later, he still had no answers. He knew that James would reach out if he could and he feared the worst. His absence only made Sam's existence in this century more unbearable.

At least once a week he rode out to East Lake Park and just walked around the resort and hoped for a miracle, but it only brought more frustration and depression.

Summer waned and the leaves turned as the night air chilled. James had now been gone for more than five months. Thanksgiving was approaching and Sam longed for his friend to share a meal with him. As the sun sank in the western sky across the lake, Sam stood on the boardwalk and thought fondly of his friend when he was startled back to reality by a voice behind him.

"Marshal, I don't know if you remember me," the young man said as Sam turned to see the red headed youngster that had pulled Joan's ancestor from the lake the day James had rescued the girl.

"Sure, you're Hiram, right?" Sam said smiling at the lad.

"I heard you been asking about that colored fellow that pulled that girl outa the lake."

"Yes, he is missing and was last seen here on the 18th of May," Sam answered trying to not get his hope up.

"Yeah... well... uhm... I saw him that night at the dummy line. These men were messing with him, and he took off running."

"Yes, I have heard that. Do you happen to know these men or know where they chased him to?"

"Uhm... naw... I mean he took off so fast I don't think they caught him... I mean I know they didn't..." his voice trailed off and his eyes were fixed on his feet.

"Why do say you know they didn't catch him?" Sam insisted.

"Well, I just know they didn't."

"Hiram, I need to know more. Do you know where he is?"

"No, sir" he answered finally looking at him again. "I promise I don't"

"Tell me what you do know. I promise you won't be in trouble. I just need to know what happened."

"You promise? You won't tell nobody?"

"I promise," Sam said excitedly. "Tell me."

The young man shuffled his feet with his hands pushed deep in his pockets as he seemed to think hard about what to say.

"Well, my Uncle Rufus... he was one of those men chasin' him... but you can't say nothing to him or nobody... you promised!"

"I promise... just tell me."

"Well, he took off runnin' and they chased after him, but he was way faster and they were about as far behind him as we are to that post yonder," he said pointing to a post on the edge of the lake about 150 feet away. "He said he took off through the old burned hotel and got right in the middle and just disappeared!"

"It was dark, so they just lost sight of him at the old hotel?"

"No, it was a full moon that night and that place is wide open. He said they could see good. He was runnin' and then about the middle of the hotel he just was gone... like a magic trick or somethin'. They went out there to make sure they wasn't seeing things to see if he just fell down or somethin' but he was gone."

"Never found him?" Sam asked to be sure.

"No sir. And Rufus swears it was magic. Said there was all this crunching sound when he was a runnin' across them charred timbers and all but when he was gone it was all quiet... not a sound."

"Anything else you can tell me, Hiram?"

"No, sir, he answered quickly and then hesitated before continuing, "I just wanted you to know I ain't like that. You know what I mean? I know it messed Rufus up. He won't even talk about it. I told him to tell you, but he said if I said anything he would whup my ass, but I thought you should know."

"Thank you. Your secret is safe with me. I appreciate you telling me."

Sam walked over to the ruins of the old hotel and surveyed the site. It was open and although the moon wasn't full tonight it was quite clear on this cloudless night. He stepped across the foundation and walked out to the middle. The charcoal crunched loudly with each step. He desperately wished for his halogen flashlight that could light up the darkest space but with just the crescent moon he couldn't really see much. He would come back in the morning to see if he could see anything that might lend any credit to the bizarre story he'd just heard.

Sam was there early the next morning and walked all over the hotel remains. He had confirmed with the bartender at the Metropolitan that the place had burned in 1891. He said the hotel was a huge structure that had already closed a few months earlier from lack of business. He said it burned to the ground in less than an hour. The fire chief reported the fire was fueled by the heart pine beams and flooring used throughout the hotel. The owner had collected a hefty insurance payout and moved up north.

Sam hadn't worked many arson cases, but he was not doubting the intensity of the fire. Now almost twenty years later, there was still little vegetation growing within the confines of the expansive foundation. The blackened charcoal beneath his boots crunched loudly with each step and he remembered Hiram's story about hearing the footsteps as James ran across. *They said he was about halfway across when he disappeared.* Sam looked as he walked but the charcoal remains all looked the same. The sun was now coming over the treetops and he could see clearly. *There is nothing here.* Then he spotted something to his left.

He walked over closer and kicked at the remains of a large timber that crumbled under his boot. *Stairwell!* Sam dropped to his knees and stuck his head over the opening that was barely visible covered in the charred remains of the old building and shouted.

"James are you there?" He shouted again and then stopped as the realization that if his friend had fallen into the abyss, it was more than four months ago. He couldn't have survived unless there was another way out. He stood and stared down to the basement floor that was at least fifteen feet below. How had the whole structure not collapsed into this basement, he thought. *Am I about to fall through?* He walked back the foundation and kicked at the brick edge and revealed the concrete floor. It was safe unless you happened to walk or run across the opening that was once the stairs into the basement.

Sam needed a ladder. He had to see if there was evidence of James falling through below. He prayed that he wouldn't find his body. He made his way back to the boat shed but the workers hadn't reported yet. He looked around for a ladder and found one, but it was only about six feet tall and would be useless for the task at hand. Then he spotted a pile of heavy rope in the corner. He picked up one end and determined it was plenty sturdy enough to hold his weight, but he was alone. How was he going to repel below by himself? Then Sam had a crazy MacGyver idea and prayed it would work.

He gathered the ladder and the rope and carried them back to the open hole. He laid the ladder across the opening and stepped carefully out on it to make sure it was capable of the task. He then kicked at the charcoal remains to uncover more of the opening and then tied the rope on two rungs of the ladder and carefully lowered himself down the hole. *This is the easy part... if there isn't another exit, will I be able to climb back out?* It was too late now, as he dropped to the floor below. The basement was more like a cellar and had once held a lot of wine, looking at the shards of glass buried with the charcoal remains. That no doubt also helped fuel the fire. Sam surveyed the room. No way out, but also... *No body, thank God!* Sam looked closely at the area below the opening and the charred remnants were all intact except for the ones bearing his boot prints. He was confident James didn't fall in here.

He walked back to the rope and looked up at the daunting target above. He grasped the rope and twisted it around his wrist as he pulled himself upward. Slowly he tugged himself to the top and grasped the ladder rung. He then took a deep breath before hoisting his lanky body up and onto the top of the prone ladder. He was thankful that his 32-year-old body was up for the task because he was sure his 58-year-old body would never have pulled off that feat. He dusted himself off and gathered the ladder and rope and returned them to the still desolate boathouse. He hadn't found James but at least he didn't find his body which he could now allow himself to admit he thought he would when he first discovered the stairwell.

On the ride back to town he replayed Hiram's account in his mind, and something struck him that he hadn't even acknowledged until this very moment. *There was a full moon!* What if James did vanish and was back home? The thought brought a smile to his face as the streetcar rambled to a stop on 2nd Avenue.

Sam couldn't possibly know if his friend had found his way home or was met with some other unimaginable demise. For now he was holding out hope for the former, but he would still keep looking although he had now exhausted every lead he had. Hopefully, he would be able to sleep tonight.

Chapter 18

Sam slept well for the first time since James disappeared. After more than eight years Sam still had trouble grasping that the flux of time was a reality. He and James had discussed the topic at length so many times, especially in those first couple of years. There was no doubt each had vivid memories of experiences and lives a century into the future, but the very idea of that still seemed preposterous. After a few years of hoping and searching for a secret portal back to the future the grim reality that they had fallen down this rabbit hole with no way back was just too painful to talk about and so any thought of it was pushed aside. But, now with James's sudden disappearance and Hiram's tale of his disappearing into thin air brought a glimmer of hope back to the surface of Sam's conscious and without James as a sounding board, it was impossible to suppress. The alternative was that James was dead, his body rotting in a shallow grave or swamp somewhere, and Sam couldn't handle that.

Sam had Christmas lunch with Conrad Austin and his family. It was good to see kids playing and to experience a family again. After lunch, Sam thanked the couple for their hospitality and took a stroll through the city. It was quiet except for the chimes ringing at St. Paul's Cathedral on the corner of 3rd Avenue and 22nd Street. There was something calming about the sound of the bells. It was familiar as Sam remembered hearing the chime during his walks through the city in 2022. The cathedral was still as magnificent more than a hundred years later.

As he passed the church, he noticed a man sitting on the porch of the rectory reading. Sam was struck by the notion that the figure relaxed on the porch swing was likely Father Coyle. Joan used the story of the father's brutal murder on that same porch in her classes. He couldn't remember when that happened... maybe the early twenties? The priest was shot on the porch by a Methodist minister who often performed weddings at the county courthouse next door. The man was part of a growing hate group focused on Catholics and anyone else that didn't look like him. He sought out the priest because he had just presided over the wedding of the minister's daughter to a Puerto Rican immigrant. It was bad enough she had married a man of color, but the fact he was Catholic was more than he could stand. He approached the priest on the porch and shot him before returning to the courthouse where he turned himself in for the crime. Months later he was found not guilty for his senseless act by a jury of his peers.

Sam knew that the murder was the result of the very hate that was just now beginning to brew in the young city and contemplated what he could do to stop it. He stood on the sidewalk staring at the priest totally emersed in whatever he was reading. He never noticed Sam's presence. Sam was overwhelmed with the sadness of his predicament and knew that nothing he could do would change the course of history.

As he passed the county courthouse, he knew that his time here had to be for a reason, but he had no idea what that was. His meeting James, a man who went through the door at the moment of his birth. James saving his life and he in turn, saving James's life. James saving Joan's great-great grandmother. *It all had to mean something, but what?*

After several more weeks, he still had no news about James and clung to the hope that he was safe, either here somewhere or in the future. It was all he had.

The new year brought more change to the city. Even more than the previous year's prohibition had. The vote for annexation of the suburban municipalities in the fall was effective on January 1st, 1910, and the city limits expanded from three square miles to more than forty-eight. The already growing population exploded from 45,000 to more than 133,000. The city was now officially described as a Metropolis as the annexations that had been almost ten years in the making became effective. The municipalities of East Lake, Avondale, Woodlawn, North Birmingham, West End, Elyton, Graymont, Pratt City and East Birmingham all became part of the city following the vote.

City Hall was now busier than ever as the Police, Fire and Administrative offices absorbed personnel from the other towns. Sam relocated his office into the Jefferson County Courthouse on 3rd Avenue. He had more space, not that he needed it, but Charles seemed pleased with the new digs.

As spring came, the politics of the city were still in flux dealing with the annexation. It seems that no one was happy regardless of what side you were on. A group was pushing to change the city government again from an Alderman system to a Commission and the newspapers were all anxious to take a side, especially if it sold more papers. In a city-wide vote on June 20th the voters chose to try the new form of government.

Soon after, the Age-Herald, the largest of the daily papers, reported that the upheaval of the metropolis annexation and changes had stressed Mayor Frank O'Brien to the point of a nervous breakdown. It was reported that the mayor was confined to home and bedrest, but Sam knew that the man had been transported to a sanitarium in Philadelphia for complete rest and quiet.

Sam kept up with his daily duties but was struggling emotionally without James. Dr. Irene Bullard had left the city following the deaths of her friends and Sam was left with just casual acquaintances to socialize with and none that he could confide in like James. He continued to walk by the blacksmith shop every evening. He took the dummy line out to East Lake Park every Wednesday night and just strolled through the park and watched the sun set over the lake.

He continued his routine and tried to find things to do to keep his mind occupied but he was miserable. He had been to a few Baron's games throughout the summer and was mesmerized by the game and how little it had changed in more than a century. The uniforms and equipment had certainly evolved but the game was the same. They did not get a new baseball every time one hit the dirt like they do in 2022, but it was a fun way to spend an evening. The park was more or less an empty lot that spanned the area between 1st Avenue and the railroad tracks. People came and stood and sat along the edges. Some brought picnic baskets. It was 1910 entertainment, simple and relaxed.

The Barons had a new owner and even though they were a minor league team, he was building a state-of-the-art steel and concrete stadium just to the west, that would be ready soon.

Opening day was August 18, and Sam was there along with more than 10,000 others. Businesses all over town were closed for the event as the Barons downed the Montgomery Climbers 3-2 in a hard-fought contest. Sam had only gone to the legendary Rickwood Field after it was refurbished in the nineties and looked forward to seeing the Barons play their annual Rickwood Classic game there each season against the current Montgomery Biscuits. He never really appreciated what the old stadium would have been like when it was new, but now it was most apparent. Watching the game, he thought about one of his favorite movies, **Field of Dreams**. He tried to remember the lines uttered by actor James Earl Jones. He had watched the movie dozens of times and knew much of the dialogue by heart. *"The one constant through all the years, Ray, has been baseball. America has rolled by like an army of steamrollers. It has been erased like a* *blackboard, rebuilt, and erased again. But baseball has marked the time.* The words were powerful the first time he watched the movie but standing here looking at this crowd and this field, that in his time was a relic, they struck him deep and tears welled in his eyes. Sam lowered his hat, wiped his eyes, and slipped out even though it was only the top of the 5th.

As the summer heat gave way to autumn, Sam continued his daily walks through the city each evening and welcomed the relief from the stifling heat since there was no air conditioning. He had now been without the modern convenience for nine years but was still not used to it.

Thanksgiving had come unceremoniously, and Christmas decorations filled the city. It was not the kind of Christmas that Sam had experienced in his 21st century life. If there was gift giving done among families it was certainly not to the extent it was in his childhood. While the newspapers had plenty of advertisements, none mentioned Santa Clause or the 'must have toy', rather the holiday seemed to be centered on families gathering. Sam didn't miss the commercial Christmases of the 21st century but he did miss gathering with friends and family and as the date approached, he missed James most of all.

On Christmas Day, Sam ate lunch in the hotel restaurant. There were only a few people there. He was sitting in the lobby reading the newspaper when he received a telegram from E.L. Higdon, Jefferson County Sheriff. Sam knew the man, but they were certainly not close. The telegram informed Sam that the sheriff was out of town and needed a favor. One of his deputies had been shot while visiting his parents last night in Oak Grove in the western part of the county. The shooter, John Laird, and his two brothers had escaped. A posse had been tracking them all night and had reason to believe they may have boarded a train in Bessemer heading to Birmingham. Higdon had a deputy stationed at the Union Station and Birmingham Police were covering the new Terminal Station. The telegram asked if he could assist the deputy at Union Station as he knew Sam lived at the hotel next door.

Sam walked into the Union Station and found the young deputy standing inside looking out at the platform. Sam approached the deputy and introduced himself.

"Good to meet you, Marshal." He said smiling, "I have heard much about you. I am Thomas Batson... just call me Tom."

Sam shook the young man's hand. He looked to be only a teenager, maybe early twenties.

"Tom, any word on the deputy that was shot?"

"No sir. Ain't looking good though. Shot him six times, they say."

"Do you know what happened?"

"He was visiting his folks for Christmas and a neighbor came over and said he heard gunshots at the Laird house next to him and asked Ollie to see what it was... Ollie Battle is the deputy... They say he went over and found John Laird standing over his daddy, dead on the floor and he shot Ollie right there. Ollie made it back outside and Laird and his brothers took off. Posse got there a couple of hours later and tracked them up to Bessemer. Some folks said they got on the train, but some said they saw them headed toward Tuscaloosa."

"You know this John Laird?" Sam asked

"No sir. They say he was in prison for almost killing a man. Ain't been out long. They say the whole family is trash. I mean him and his brothers, always in trouble with the law. I only been a deputy since July, so I don't know them. I usually work the north end of the county serving papers and such."

Sam had his doubts that three outlaws fleeing would board a train, but he had enough experience to know that criminals often did stupid things. Union Station had lost most of its passenger service to the new Terminal Station. The only passenger trains using the station now were the L & N and Atlanta, Birmingham & Atlantic Railway (AB&A), although often other trains would make a stop here to off load packages, mail, and other cargo before heading across to the new Terminal Station for passengers to disembark. No doubt, the sheriff had assigned the rookie deputy here just in case they slipped off the train and had the bigger presence of the BPD at the Terminal Station. Sam thought it was unlikely the men were even on a train but kept his thoughts to himself and waited with the young deputy.

Within a few minutes the train arrived, and the passengers remained aboard while workers offloaded mail bags and some freight items in the rear. Sam and Tom stood on the platform looking for anything suspicious but as Sam had predicted no one left the train. The conductor noticed the pair and asked if they were looking for something on the train.

"Three outlaws that may have gotten on in Bessemer," Sam said. "Looks like they were wrong though."

"I just run three scoundrels out of the freight car when we pulled in. Hiding in the back," the conductor said pointing to the car.

"Where?" Sam said, "I didn't see anyone come through."

"They went up the street that way," he said pointing out toward Morris and 20th."

"What were they wearing?" Sam shouted as he headed toward the doors with the deputy on his heels.

"One had a brown shirt and red hair," he said as the two lawmen went out the door. Sam ran to the corner. The streets were almost completely empty, but he caught a glimpse of someone rounding the corner onto 1st Avenue in front of the construction site and he and the deputy followed.

The sun was bright, and the air was crisp as the law men reached 1st Avenue, they didn't need a description of the bad guys as shots rang out from the east and Sam saw the wooden post on the scaffolding beside him splinter. The three brothers stood abreast across the sidewalk their guns blazing. Sam instinctively returned fire taking cover behind the scaffolding that wasn't really cover at all. His first bullet struck the middleman in the chest, and he saw him fall as he felt the hot lead tear into the star on his chest and rip though his body. The deputy fired and hit one of the others in the thigh and he went to the ground. Sam felt the searing pain rushing through his body as he fired two rounds at the man on his right and saw the bullets strike the target and blood explode from his chest and neck. Sam hit the ground hard and saw that the deputy was prone beside him, bleeding from his right arm. His gun was lying on the sidewalk beside him as he gripped the wound with his left hand. Sam then saw the man with the leg wound taking aim and he fired two more rounds and saw him drop to the sidewalk. Sam could hear the young deputy screaming in agony and tried to comfort him, but words wouldn't come. He was cold lying on the sidewalk looking up at the building that would become the John Hand Building almost a century later. It was only two stories tall now and surrounded by scaffolding. The bright sun was reflecting off the limestone façade he could see through the wooden scaffold. It was really cold, and his vision blurring. He was losing consciousness. *This is how it ends.* He tried to reach out to the deputy, but everything faded to black. It was black and silent, and Sam finally felt at peace.

Chapter 19

The silence was broken by a loud beeping sound. Sam was still cold, but his vision returned, although still blurry. He could feel his body being jostled but it was like he was in some altered state. He could sense the movement but couldn't feel his own body. He tried to open his eyes, but the sun was now directly overhead and brighter than ever. He tried to focus. The beeping continued incessantly. He could see the limestone façade of the John Hand Building again but there was no scaffolding, and he was now staring at the 21-story building fully complete.

"Marshal, can you hear me?" A voice rang out that sounded as though it came from the depths of an echo chamber, both muffled and loud at the same time. "Marshal, blink your eyes if you can hear me."

A young African American man's face now interrupted the view of the building beside him. A stethoscope hung from his ears as he spoke, "Marshal, can you hear me?"

"Yes, I can hear you," Sam said in almost a whisper. He barely recognized his own voice.

"We are going to transport you now. You hang on. Try to stay awake for me."

Sam still couldn't feel his body although he sensed the movement and was loaded into the ambulance. The voices were muffled but the beeping was annoyingly loud. He was trying to remember what happened, but it was all foggy. *Train. Deputy. Shooting. I was shot!* He was tired, so tired. He just wanted to sleep.

"Stay with me, Marshall."

The voice kept repeating almost in synch with the damn beeping. It was as if he was awakening from a deep sleep that he could just not conquer. *Sirens... I hear sirens!* He could not conquer the need for rest, and all faded to black.

"Sam, can you wake up for me?"

He tried to respond but his eyelids were so heavy. He felt a soft hand on his face and tried to reach up to feel it, but his arms felt like they weighed a ton. He struggled again to open his eyes and could only see the fuzzy glow from overhead lights as a face leaned in. It was a woman wearing a funny green covering on her head and a surgical mask on her face. Her blue eyes were kind.

"Sam, I am Valerie, and I am going to take care of you. You are in recovery. Your surgery went well. Can you talk?"

"Where am I?" was all Sam could muster. His voice was hoarse, and his throat was raw.

"You're at UAB Medical Center, Sam. You were shot but you're going to be okay. You just need to rest. The anesthesia will be clearing soon, and you'll feel better."

Sam closed his eyes and tried to clear his mind from the cobwebs. *Train. Deputy. Shooting.* He remembered walking into the ambush.

"Is Tom okay?" Sam asked still trying to fill in the gaps in his memory, but he remembered the rookie sprawled bleeding on the sidewalk beside him.

"I'm not sure who Tom is, Sam?" the nurse responded, again stroking his face.

"He was the deputy sheriff with me," Sam said. The simple sentence took all of his energy to mutter.

"I'll check but you were the only patient so I think he must be okay."

Sam kept trying to piece together the events, but he was so tired he could no longer fight it. He needed sleep.

"Sam we are moving you up to the 9th floor. They will take great care of you up there, okay?"

Sam tried to respond but he was so tired. His left shoulder now felt like it was in a vice. He tried his best to wake up but just couldn't manage more than a few seconds before succumbing to sleep again.

Sam woke up in the ICU with a man in blue scrubs at his bedside.

"Sam, my name is Jason. I'm your nurse. How are you feeling?"

"Like I've been shot," Sam quipped with his hoarse voice, although he was still trying to get his bearings. He remembered the shootout. He remembered waking up after surgery and being told he was at UAB, but he felt like that was a lifetime ago.

"Well, you were shot, but you are on the mend now. You've been pretty groggy since you came up from surgery. Are you feeling better?"

"Maybe, it's hard to tell. How long have I been here?"

"You've been in the ICU for about seven hours now," Jason said as he glanced through the chart. "My shift just started... looks like you were in the ED for a about three hours and then in surgery for five before they brought you up. Your vitals are good. But you tell me how you feel on a scale of one to ten?" he said pointing at the large whiteboard at the foot of the bed with a pain chart labeled with both numbers and smiley faces.

"Pain is okay, but I'm still trying to sort things out," he admitted out loud as his brain worked overtime.

"I'm glad your pain is better. You've experienced a serious trauma, so confusion is nothing to worry about... the fog will clear... just give it some time."

"Can you tell me what day it is?" Sam asked.

"It's Saturday," the nurse responded pointing again to the whiteboard -- Saturday, October 29, 2022. Sam gasped aloud and startled the nurse.

"What's wrong, Sam?"

"Ummm... nothing. Sorry," Sam said apologetically.

"That didn't sound like nothing to me. Are you in pain?"

"Not really. My shoulder feels like it's in a vice or something."

"It's immobilized so you don't move that arm. Your wound is packed and stabilized. The doctor will look at it later today. He will likely have us clean it up. Is that the only thing bothering you right now?"

"Yes, I'm okay," Sam said weighing his options in his mind. His brain was still foggy, but he knew that if he started talking about spending the last ten years in the previous century and being shot in 1910, he would go straight from the ICU to the Psych ward. *I've got to get my head straight... THINK!* Sam's mind was spinning as his nurse entered data in the computer and went in and out of the glass door beside his bed. He was never far away.

Sam replayed the day's events. He got the telegram. Went across the street to the train station. Met the rookie deputy, Tom Batson. They chased after the outlaws and met a hail of gunfire when they turned the corner on 1st Avenue. He winced as he remembered the hot lead tearing into his chest and looked down to see the wad of gauze and tape above his left breast. *Did I die?*

He thought about his entire ordeal. He looked at the date on the whiteboard again. It was the day after he went through the door. He looked at the clock over the board – 04:12 AM – *So I came back on the same day I left! Was that all a dream or am I really crazy?*

Jason returned carrying a small cup of crushed ice. "Eat this slowly, it'll make your throat feel better," he said returning to his tablet and typing more.

"Can you tell me what I was wearing when they brought me in?" Sam asked.

"Let's see," the nurse answered opening a small cabinet door on the back wall and retrieving a large plastic bag. "Looks like the police kept your shirt and jacket. There is a receipt here. Jeans and Nike shoes and your underwear. It's all pretty bloody though," he said holding the bag up. "If you had any valuables in your pockets, they have them in the safe... looks like a wallet with three cards and $845 cash, iPhone and iWatch... does that sound right?"

"Yeah, that sounds right," Sam answered and fed that data into everything running through his mind. That was everything he had when he went through the door but when he was shot, he maybe had $30 in his pocket and that damn pocket watch. *Did all this happen in my brain? NO! It was too real and took too damn long! It had to be real.*

Sam needed answers but just like the night he met James, he would need to figure this out on his own. He remembered the King novel and when his characters came back to the present only 2 minutes had passed, no matter how long they had been in the past. *Nothing else every worked though, no magic portal. It is fiction and this is real. None of this makes sense. For ten years none of this has made sense.*

The nurse was checking the IV in his right hand and Sam looked at the back of his hand where the IV had been inserted. Then he looked at the other hand. The small brown spots were there. He looked at his faint reflection in the glass wall beside his bed. His hair was mostly white. The 32-year-old version was definitely gone.

His brain fog was now clearer, and he thought about all the events he'd experienced during those ten years stuck there. *There is too much... too many details... it cannot all be in my head.* He thought about being shot and all that went with it. He remembered the last time he'd been shot and tried to wrestle the sheet off his right leg.

"Hey, what do you need?" Jason said rushing to the bedside.

"Sorry, I just wanted to look at my leg."

"Is something wrong?"

"No, I was just shot there years ago," he explained as the nurse pulled back the sheet exposing the circular scar above his knee surrounded by surgical incision scars.

"Looks like they did good work," Jason said. "Don't look at that chest wound. It's a bit nastier right now but it will look better soon."

Sam's brain was working overtime as he ran through the list of coincidences experienced during his time in the past century – James going through the door on his birthday, James saving his life in the shootout with the Hill boys and then him saving James. James saving Joan's great-great grandmother as a child. James's disappearance. *Did he make it back too?*

Sam lay in the ICU replaying the last nine years in his mind and was convinced more than ever that it could not have been a dream or just in his mind. *Too many details*. It was just too real, yet here he was just hours after he went through the door. If that was all brought on by the trauma of being shot, why can't I remember that shooting? The nurse had mentioned that the police had asked to interview him as soon as he felt like talking. He knew he was not going to be any help as he had no recollection, and he wasn't about to start talking about walking into the ambush of the Laird brothers in 1910. He wouldn't be any help to their investigation but maybe they could tell him something that would trigger a memory or something that would make any of this make sense. Right now, he was exhausted from all the thinking and slipped back to a restful sleep.

He woke up to the smell of food and was suddenly starving. The mushy scrambled eggs and grits looked much less appetizing than they smelled but Sam inhaled them along with the toast and apple jelly.

"Well, I see your appetite is back," Jason quipped as he cleared the tray. "Can I get you something else?"

"Anyway I can get a Coke?" Sam asked.

"Sure, I'll be right back with one. By the way, the detectives are here if you feel like talking."

"Yeah, sure... still don't remember anything, but I can talk."

Sam took a big swig of the Coke and almost spit it out. It was vastly different from the concoction in the green bottle he had become accustomed to drinking every morning. But for air conditioning and other amenities, he would learn to like this one.

A young African American came in through the glass door with his badge and credentials in his hand. "Marshal Robbins, I'm Detective Sergeant Micah Williamson with Birmingham PD. Do you feel up to answering some questions?"

"Sure, but I have no recollection of being shot or anything that may have led up to it," Sam said apologetically.

"That's okay, tell me what you do remember."

"That's just it. I don't remember anything. I remember getting breakfast at June's and heading out for a walk down Morris and nothing beyond that... not sure if it was the same day even... sorry. Can you tell me what happened?"

"Well, I would rather you try and remember all you can about yesterday morning..."

"GODDAMN MAN! He is a fucking cop!" the interrupting voice boomed and reverberated off the glass walls as Sergeant Zeke Adams appeared in the door. "Give him a fucking break, man! He was shot in the fucking chest! He can't remember. He ain't a suspect for God's sake. I worked with this man for twenty years, don't be an asshole!" Adams anger switched immediately to a huge grin as reached out and grabbed Sam's right hand gently.

"How are you, brother?" he asked. Zeke Adams was an African American man who had been Sam's partner in homicide for more than ten years. At 6'6" tall and 290 pounds he was a bit taller than Sam and about twice as wide. His bald head gleamed under the overhead lights. He wore his familiar attire, a short-sleeve dress shirt, clip-on tie, and black slacks. His smile and voice both commanded attention.

"Except for being shot and having no memories of it, I guess I am okay," Sam said looking at his friend.

"That's good. You will have to forgive my colleague from the Robbery Unit. He is new, and he is by the book, and he's not yet learned his manners," he said turning to look scornfully at the young man.

The younger detective became silent and stepped back as far as he could which was only one step from the pair, but he remained silent.

"Here is what we know, Sam. Evidently, these hombres had just robbed an investment bank office of some bearer bonds in the John Hand Building. I didn't even know there was a fucking bank still in that building. It ain't a real bank like me or you would use, but anyway, they make their exit, and the security guard encounters them on the first floor as they are about to exit, and they pop a cap or two and he hits the floor. The 911 call has already gone out and they head out on foot toward Morris with the security guard following but not chasing. Then they encounter you. Not sure if you saw their weapons or what, but they do a 180 and head back toward first. Witnesses say that when you turned the corner, they started shooting. You got both of them and one of them evidently got you too. You remember any of that?"

"No," was all Sam could manage as the description was racing through his brain. "So, I was carrying?"

"Evidently. Your U.S. Marshal official Glock," Zeke assured him. "You also had your star in your left hand, so obviously you had identified yourself. Nothing?"

"I'm sorry. I don't remember anything. Aren't I retired?" He asked, hoping that this too wasn't some fact thwarted by centuries and timelines.

Zeke laughed loudly. "Not officially, my man! You have been off for a couple of weeks, but you got almost a month of vacation time to burn before you can officially hang it up again! Don't tell me you don't remember your party next Friday? You got to get outta here, man! I would hate to have a party for you without your ass being there! Joan will be pissed if you mess up the party," he laughed again.

The mention of her name sent a cold shiver down Sam's spine. "Joan?"

"Yeah, man. I forgot she's been waiting on us. We need to wrap this up so she can get in here. You done, Williamson?" Zeke asked the silent young detective.

"Uhhh... yeah... call me if you remember anything," the young detective said placing his card on the tray table by the bed.

"Man, I am glad to see you survive another one... You get well and I will see you soon," Zeke beamed as the pair slipped into the unit through the glass wall.

Joan is alive and here? My brain is definitely fucked up. Sam was both elated and scared hearing the news. *Did I dream that Joan died too?* His mind raced with all the thoughts and memories of Joan's illness and her death. A wave of emotions swelled as he tried to make any sense of it all.

Within a few seconds, the love of his life was passing by the glass wall and then at his bedside. Her face showed the grave concern and the sheer joy at seeing him alive. Her hair was long, thick, and a beautiful silver white. Her figure was full, and her face was beautiful. His last memory of her was bald, rail thin, her skin yellow and eyes vacant. He could not say anything. He sobbed as she leaned in, and he hugged her tight with his one arm for several minutes.

"Oh my God! You look great. I expected the worst," she admitted. "I thought I was going to have to fight them. They wouldn't let me in until the cops interviewed you. I caught just a glimpse of you as they wheeled you to surgery. I thought I had lost you," she said kissing him on the face and then deeply on the mouth.

Sam was so overwhelmed he still couldn't find words. What would he tell her? *Of all the weird shit that has happened to me this is by far the very best.* He tightened his hug.

"I just want to hold you," was all he could say.

Chapter 20

When Sam finally released his grip, Joan looked in his eyes with concern, "How are you really doing?"

"Physically, I'm okay... for a guy that's been shot in the chest," he said with a slight smile that seemed to relieve some of the tension in Joan's face.

"Something is wrong. You know I can tell," she said almost whispering.

"Yeah, I am okay, but I have so much to tell you. I have had the craziest dream or hallucination but if I tell you, you have to promise not to send me to the nut house, okay?"

"Okay, but they are going to be transferring you to a regular room as soon as they have one available. I talked to the surgeon and your doctor while I was waiting for them to let me in. No idea how long but they said it shouldn't be too long."

"It can wait. I don't even know where to start anyway," he said and considered his next words carefully. "My brain is foggy. I have no recall of the shooting. Zeke told me what happened, but I don't remember anything. In my dream, or whatever it was, you died of cancer, and I was alone..." he couldn't finish the words and tears streamed down his face. Joan bent over to hold him again.

"I had breast cancer four years ago and was pretty sick. Do you remember that?"

Sam nodded as the dreaded memories and grief came flooding back again.

"My doctor enrolled me in a study here at UAB -- experimental treatments but it worked. Eight months later I was back at work!"

Sam was trying to process the news and had no recollection of any experimental treatment being offered.

"You don't remember that do you?"

"No... it was so real."

Joan hugged him again and kissed his face and wiped away the tears. "I am so sorry, but I am fine... cancer-free for over three years."

Jason reappeared with another nurse or technician and informed them that he was being transferred to the Trauma Step-Down Unit down the hall. He handed Joan the plastic bag with the jeans and shoes in it.

"Sam, you get well. I don't want to hear any reports of you harassing the staff down there. They won't be in your business as much as I was, but they'll take great care of you."

"Thanks," Sam said as he was wheeled out of the ICU with Joan following behind.

Once they were settled in the room, Joan pulled the chair close to the bed and sat holding Sam's hand.

"I know your dream was upsetting, but don't worry about it or your memory loss. We will talk to the doctor, but I am sure it's the trauma and nothing to worry about. We have to get you well before February... do you remember we are going to Paris?"

"No, I don't remember that, but it sounds wonderful," Sam said and squeezed Joan's hand. This was all so surreal. It was almost like being suddenly thrust into 1901 was. His memories of his nine years there were so vivid and yet it seems the years leading up to his going through the door had now been altered or was it all in his head. *Joan was alive and well! What else had changed.*

"Don't freak out when I ask, but my memories are really jumbled up. The dream was so real but so are my memories leading up to it, like your getting sick and my losing you. Yet other memories are so clear. I remember getting shot in 2012. Was that real?"

"Yes, too real."

"I remember that in vivid detail, but nothing about how this happened," he said looking at the bandages on his chest and shoulder.

"Don't worry. We will sort through it," Joan reassured him. "As bad as that shooting was, this was much worse. There was a brief moment where we thought you might lose your leg and then most of the doctors assured me your career was over but yet you were back on the job in less than a year. But this time, they had to resuscitate you four different times. First on the sidewalk and then in the ambulance and twice more after you arrived here. Plus, I know you don't want to hear it but you're older now," she smiled.

"Yes, I am. They say you're only as old as you feel and right now that might be about 200 or so," he joked. They sat in silence for a few moments as Sam tried to come up with the best way to tell her. *Why is this so hard? We have always talked about everything. No secrets.* But they had never had anything like this. Finally, Sam decided there was no easing into this. He just had to lay it out.

"You know we've always been honest with each other, and I need to tell you about this dream or whatever it was, and maybe I need to see a shrink or something, but I want you to hear it first, okay?"

"Tell me. I told you, we will work through this."

"I really don't know where to start, but we've talked a little about what I don't remember but let me tell you what I do remember and obviously you will see some of these memories are not factual, starting with your illness and death. I can fill in vivid details but let me just run through it."

Joan squeezed his hand and leaned in with a compassionate look in her eyes.

"I remember the day at the hospital when you died. I remember your memorial service. I remember the weeks and months afterward. I moved downtown and tried to start over. I cancelled my plans to retire and worked for two more years before finally doing it." Joan just listened and rubbed his arm as he continued.

"On the 28th of October I got up and ate breakfast at June Coffee and went for my morning walk like had been doing for the last two weeks since I retired... this is where the crazy begins," he warned but Joan just gave him a reassuring nod and he continued.

"I am going west on Morris, and I notice a door ajar on the Arrington overpass that I had never before noticed, and I stop to investigate. I looked in but it was completely dark, so I pulled out my iPhone to shine a light in to see what it was. Then I was hit with this intense light and the temp dropped to freezing cold. I got disoriented and couldn't find the door even though I was only a step inside. Then everything started to spin, and I blacked out. I woke up in the middle of the street staring up at the full moon. I was still on Morris but there were no overpasses. I was now dressed in old clothes; my phone was now a pocket watch and I found out later that it was still October 28th, only it was 1901!" Joan didn't say anything but just continued to listen as Sam told her about James finding him and then later revealing that he too had come from the future in the same manner in 1963. He told her how their friendship grew but they had to meet secretly because of the race relations at the time. He told her about James saving her great-great grandmother as a child and finally Joan reacted with an audible gasp. Sam stopped and looked at her.

"My grandmother told me a story of how her grandmother almost drowned in East Lake when she was a little girl. She was terrified of water, and that fear passed down through the generations. My mom was the first person in the family to learn to swim and she never told her mom," Joan said as she recalled her past. "But I don't think I've ever told you that."

"I don't remember you telling me that and in my dream I went to the courthouse and looked up birth records and confirmed it was your family."

He went on to tell her that about the tension and threats afterward and of James's disappearance. Then he told her of Christmas Day 1910 when he rounded the same corner on 1st Avenue where Zeke described him being shot and met a hail of gunfire from John Laird and his brothers and then woke up here.

"I was there for over nine years, and I have distinct memories of my daily life there. It was pretty miserable, but James had it much worse. We searched diligently for a couple of years to find some secret passage back but eventually gave up and decided that if we ever made it back it wouldn't be up to us... it would just happen the way it did when we went back. Do you think I'm crazy?"

"No! I don't. You had a very traumatic experience. You know you read stories of people seeing the light and seeing dead relatives and such, but I've never thought they were crazy. The brain is a powerful thing that we know so little about. You are not crazy. We will work through this, I promise," she said standing up and leaning in to kiss him softly. "You're going to be okay."

"It's all so crazy. It was so real and so long, but it was worth it all to have you back. Tell me more about Paris and about us after you beat the cancer."

Joan sat back down and leaned in, still holding his hand, "When I was first diagnosed, we finally got off the bubble and moved downtown. Do you remember that?"

"In my brain, I moved after your death."

"Well, after I went back to work, we were both still planning to retire but Mac convinced you to stay on until the trails were over in the Governor's corruption case. Do you remember?"

"Yes, but after I was alone. I kind of threw myself into work."

"I took on more classes and postponed the retirement to the end of this year. You were burning your vacation time and had been home for a couple of weeks and I have two more weeks of classes before I am officially retired. We have a month-long trip planned for February starting in Paris, then on to London and Scotland. So, you have got to get well!"

Sam smiled and relished the thoughts of spending time with Joan who he thought was lost forever. Just as it was so hard to fathom his arrival in 1901 Birmingham, he was finding his return to 2022 just as unbelievable. *Did history change somehow while I was gone or was it really all just in my brain?* He thought about his first few months in 1901 and how he hoped it was all a dream or due to a head injury but that faded with time, and it all became real when James told him about his story. Now he was having difficulty believing that it wasn't real. It was all just too real. He may never figure it out, but the most important thing was he had Joan back and that was all that really mattered. He drifted off to sleep with that contentment.

Chapter 21

Sam awoke to the smell of food. He looked up to see Joan beside him arranging food on his tray.

"Lunch time?"

"I am afraid you slept through lunch, so I had Full Moon delivered. You are getting well because you woke up as soon as it arrived! Are you hungry?"

"Yes, I am. I haven't had barbeque in almost ten years," he joked.

Joan smiled and was glad to see he was trying to cope with his confusion and the dream. She placed the food and pushed the tray over his bed.

"The surgeon checked in on you while you were napping but said he would be back around five."

Sam looked at the clock and it was almost four in the afternoon. He had slept almost six hours and he finally felt rested. His shoulder and arm twinged a bit but not enough to keep him from sleeping. The pain meds probably helped with that. The pulled pork sandwich, potato salad and baked beans were heavenly.

After eating, Joan pulled out her iPad and showed Sam their vacation itinerary including photos of their hotels. He was lost in the thought of time spent with her. Time, he thought he'd never have. Any thoughts of the 1900's were pushed aside. *I need to give it a break. If I keep dwelling on that I can't enjoy this.* He was determined to make the most of this second chance, even if it wasn't really a second chance anywhere but his mind. Even if it wasn't real, there is no doubt, he had a near death experience, and it was a second chance for him.

The tour of Europe was interrupted with a visit from the attending doctor followed by two others that were either interns or students. Sam wasn't sure from the introductions. All he caught was the attending's name, Debra Clarkson. She looked at his chart and checked his wound before placing her stethoscope just below the wound and then on the side of his neck.

"Mr. Robbins, you are doing great. The wound is healing nicely, and your heart and blood flow are back to normal. That bullet just missed your heart and the aorta but as you can imagine it came close enough to put some major stress on it. As they probably told you, it quit working and didn't want to start back but the doctors in the ED finally got you back and the surgical team got you patched up and everything now is good. I want you to rest here one more day and get a good run of antibiotics in, but we can send you home by tomorrow afternoon, I think. Do you have any questions?"

"No, thanks doctor," was all that Sam could come up with. It was all too weird and unreal still.

"What will he need when we go home?" Joan asked knowing that she would be the caregiver once they were out of the hospital.

"He shouldn't need too much. PT will be by later today and get him to start moving the shoulder, but it doesn't look like it was adversely affected. It will be tender, of course, but he should have full range of motion once it heals completely. We will send you home with a course of antibiotics, but he is already off the pain meds now. So, in a week or so he will need to come in for stich removal and to let us check everything. The internal sutures will dissolve. By Thanksgiving he will be well on the way to normal and by Christmas he will be as good as new."

Only minutes after the doctors left the physical therapist showed up with two trainees in tow. After getting Sam sitting on the side of the bed, he removed the strapping that secured Sam's left arm to his side and had him slowly lift the arm. It was fine to a point but when it hit that point, a bolt of pain shot through his body.

"Yes, that is your body saying that is enough!" he explained. "Every couple of hours I want you to raise the arm as far as you can to the front, then to the back like this and then out to the side." Sam followed the guidance and moved the arm in all three positions. All to the point of searing pain.

"Now here is the tough part. Each time I want you to push just beyond that pain point. You will find that with each session you will be able to go a little farther. By the time we check on you in the morning, you will be able to raise it a lot higher. Don't go too far but just a couple inches past where it's uncomfortable, okay?"

"Thanks," Sam said as he moved the arm in small circles.

"It feels good just to get that strap off, doesn't it?"

"Yes, it does."

"While we are here, do you feel like standing up? Let's get you moving a bit and make sure your balance is okay?"

Sam stood and his legs were a bit shaky but then steadied as the other two people stood at his sides.

"Let's just walk across the room to me over here," the therapist said as he stepped over to the edge of the room in front of the window. The first step was a little precarious but then Sam felt almost normal as he slowly walked toward the young man as his two guards shadowed him. One was rolling the IV pole with each step.

"Excellent. You've got this! Get up as often as you can but let your nurse know so they can help, okay? Your strength is good."

Sam reached his destination and peered out at the sprawling medical center beneath him. The city looked so different. Some many buildings everywhere. Then he spotted the little red brick building on the next block. It was mostly obscured by other buildings, but he recognized it although he could only see the roof and top floor windows. It was the original Hillman Hospital. It looked so different snuggled in amidst the tall building surrounding it. It had looked so much bigger as it stood alone on the corner.

Sam made the return trip to the bed without any problem. When they were alone, he told Joan about visiting her great-great grandmother in the hospital and meeting her aunt Joan and the uncanny resemblance to her.

"The hospital was brand new. I watched them building it and was there when they opened," he said. "Or least I had a very realistic dream about it."

Joan stood at the window looking out as he described the events.

"You didn't say anything to the doctor about my confusion or the dream," Sam said finally.

"Let's give it some time. If you want to talk to a professional, we can find someone. If that's what you want."

She walked back to the bedside and took his hand and sat on the edge of the bed.

"You're still not sure it was a dream, are you?"

Sam looked into her soft green eyes and shook his head. "I am not sure of anything... except you. It was so real, and I have ten years of memories with vivid details, but then here I am, and I have no memory of the events that put me here."

"We will sort it out, just give it some time. Let's get your body healed. Things may clear when you get back home."

The conversation was interrupted by rap on the door as the surgeon came in.

"Mr. Robbins, my name is Dr. Lewis, and I was one of the surgeons that worked on you. How are you feeling."

"Much better," Sam answered fixated on the embroidered name above the pocket of the white lab coat the surgeon wore over his green scrubs – Dr. J.R. Lewis III, M.D.

"That's great to hear," he said as he lifted the bandage slightly and shined a pen light to see the sutured wound on his chest. "Can you sit up for me?" He repeated the procedure looking at the exit wound on his back.

"Any unusual pain or anything?"

"No, just a little stiff," was all Sam could offer still staring at the name. His skin was much lighter than James's and he had a head full of hair,

209

but what are the chances his surgeon would have the same last name? *One more unexplained coincidence?*

"Well, that will ease soon as the swelling goes down. I would say that you are a lucky man but no one who gets shot in the chest is really lucky. The bullet did miraculously miss your heart by about two centimeters and your aorta by even less."

"So, I am told. I'm thankful for you all saving me."

"Unfortunately, I see too many gunshot wounds but yours is perplexing. The gun that shot you was a modern Sig -- a semi-auto. Did you know that?"

"No, I don't have any memory of the shooting. Just what Zeke told me."

"Oh, yes, you were a Birmingham Detective before becoming a Marshal, right?"

"Yes, twenty-five years. Zeke was my partner for about ten of those."

"Right. Here is the perplexing part... the exit wound is really small, which tells me that it wasn't a jacketed bullet. I pulled three tiny fragments of lead out of you, but I am not sure they were large enough for the lab to get anything. Your wound was more like ones I've seen from old revolvers... you know old cast lead bullets at low velocity. It's just kind of strange, but everything looks good and you're already healing nicely."

Sam had visions of the blazing cowboy guns as he turned that corner... *they certainly weren't jacketed bullets. Another coincidence?*

"That is strange... I'm just glad you could fix me up."

"Any chance there are more fragments still in there?" Joan asked with a worried look.

"There is always a chance, but it would be very unlikely and if there were it would be so small that any damage it could do would be very unlikely. We didn't find anything else in the x-rays."

"I know, I have already said this, but I will keep saying it, thank you again for everything!" Joan added shaking the young doctor's hand.

"Okay. I will leave you to rest. Do you have any more questions?"

"This is totally unrelated, and none of my business," Sam said, "but I knew a Dr. Lewis years ago... are you from Birmingham?"

"Yes, I am!" the young doctor answered with a big smile. "What was your doctor's first name... do you know?"

"Yes, James," Sam answered.

"You can see I am the third," he said pointing to his name on the lab coat. "James Raymond... Both my dad... junior... and my grandfather are physicians. I grew up in Homewood. Went to Med school here then moved off to New York for a few years, married a New Yorker and brought her back to the south."

"Are they still alive?" Sam asked trying to not be too excited.

"Yes, my dad is a cardiac surgeon here and my granddad just retired a couple of years ago at the age of 80. He was an oncologist here."

"Oh my God!" Joan exclaimed, "He was my oncologist on the genome team."

"You're a breast cancer survivor?"

"Yes, I was in the trial for the genome therapy, and it saved my life."

"My grandfather pioneered that program... that is why he worked until he was eighty. He wanted to see it come to fruition. They are actually honoring him tomorrow and are naming the new cancer center for him. If you don't mind, I will bring him by to see you... he will love hearing from you."

"Oh, I would love that... I only saw him once briefly, but his team was so awesome."

"Ceremony is at ten so we will drop in on our way over. I am off tomorrow but that will give me a chance to check on this guy too," he said nodding at Sam.

Sam was doing the math in his head. This guy was no more than thirty-five, so his dad would be too young, but an eighty-year-old grandfather would be about the same age as James. *Maybe he did make it back.*

Chapter 22

Sam slept in shifts after insisting that Joan go home, and she finally relented just before midnight. Besides the noise and activity of being in a hospital, he couldn't stop thinking about the young surgeon and the possibility that his grandfather could be James. *If it is him, will he recognize me? The fifty-eight-year-old me looks quite a bit different from the thirty-two-year-old me. Did he come back to 1963 or some other time?* It was all too confusing. Too many possibilities. And how did he explain all the changes he came back to?

The logical explanation was that the entire events he remembers of being in the 1900's were all in his brain, a result of the trauma suffered from being shot in the chest and dying for brief periods of time. The name Lewis was just another coincidence that his brain has woven into this detailed memory or fantasy or nightmare. At times it was all three of those things.

He woke up from one of his many naps to find Joan back at his bedside. It was 06:43 according to the clock at the end of his bed. She said that she did manage to sleep some and was glad to find him in good spirits. Sam sat up on the side of his bed and Joan guided him to the bathroom. His IV had been removed during one of the nightly visits, so he was now untethered. He peed and then splashed cold water on his face. He felt a lot better than he looked, he thought as he looked at the old man staring back at him in the mirror. He sat in the chair beside the window and moved his arm and found the PT guy was correct, his movements were increased by more than fifty percent after several rounds of movement. Joan was almost as excited about meeting the surgeon's grandfather as Sam was but for different reasons. She confessed to Sam that she was on the verge of giving up when she got into the study group. Her prognosis had been dire from the time the cancer was discovered and nothing seemed to quell its aggressive nature until she started the genome therapy.

At just past nine, a rap on the door came followed by the entrance of the young surgeon, now dressed in a smart blue suit and white shirt with a perfectly tied bow tie. He was followed by and elderly gentleman in a dark grey suit and wire rimmed spectacles. He was much slimmer than the James of 1900. Probably by fifty pounds or more. Still, Sam thought he could see some vague resemblance of his friend in the elderly gent with the slightly stooped posture, but he couldn't be sure, and the old man showed no sign of recognizing him.

"Joan and Sam, this is my grandfather, the distinguished Dr. James R. Lewis, Sr. Granddad, this is Joan Robbins, that I told you about and this is her husband, Sam."

"Joan, it is a pleasure to see you again and I hope I am not out of line by saying you look much better than the last time we met," he smiled and took Joan's hand.

Sam sat mesmerized at the booming baritone voice coming from the old man. It had to be James, but he showed no sign of recognition of Sam.

"I feel much better, too!" she said with a laugh.

"And Sam, it is a pleasure to see you also. I hear you had some trouble dodging a bullet!"

"That's what they tell me and the hole in my chest and back seem to back that up," he said looking deep into his dark brown eyes. There seemed to be no glimmer of recognition on his part. "Are you planning to go back to being a Marshal or are you going to hang up your spurs."

"Oh, I am done. Retirement papers were filed already."

"Gran, we need to get downstairs, we can't have you missing your own ceremony," the surgeon said, and the pair moved toward the door.

"Thanks for allowing me to intrude," the old fellow said as he reached the door.

"Oh, it was our pleasure," Joan said, "Thank you so much and congratulations on an honor well deserved."

"Thank you," he said. "I have been very blessed in my life. Mostly to see my children and grandchildren all grow up and prosper. Sam, you take care of this young lady and cherish your time with her."

"I certainly will."

As the old man went through the door, Sam was already trying to process the meeting and his disappointment when the man peered around the almost closed door and placed his index finger beside his nose and looked directly at Sam before disappearing again.

Epilogue

Sam was waiting outside John's City Diner when the hostess opened the doors at 11. The lunch he and James had scheduled more than a month ago wasn't until 11:30 but he was so anxious he couldn't wait.

He sat a booth near the back sipping his iced tea and stared at the door awaiting James's arrival. At 11:25, he saw the slender man enter. He was certainly elderly but looked and moved like a much younger man. Dressed in jeans and a bright green sweater, he smiled as he spotted Sam and headed toward him. The two men embraced in a bear hug for several seconds before taking their seats.

After their encounter in the hospital, James had sent a note to Sam explaining that he was leaving on a long vacation to Europe the following day and asked that they meet at the diner when he returned to catch up. Sam had shown the note to Joan and spent the next four weeks doing his physical therapy and regaining his strength, while telling Joan all the tales of his weird adventure back in time. He wasn't sure she was convinced that it really happened, but she seemed content. He counted down the days until he could reunite with his friend.

James explained that as he was being chased by a group of angry men from the train stop in East Lake, he was running across the burned ruins of the old hotel heading for the woods behind it hoping to lose the men when he suddenly felt himself falling. "It was as if I had stepped off an abyss. Then, just like going through the door, it was freezing cold and spinning and seconds later I landed on my feet," James explained. "The first thing I noticed was my shoes. They were the ones I was wearing when I went through the door. I found myself on the bridge almost directly above the spot I where I went through the door. The city was dark, but the moon was bright, a full moon!"

Sam sat taking in the story and thought about the night James went missing and his agony in the days and weeks following his disappearance wondering what his fate might be.

"I made my way back to the Greyhound station, but it was deserted and so I headed over to the Gaston motel, figuring if it was the same night I disappeared, that's where everyone would be. As I got there, I saw my uncle's car and he was asleep in the driver's seat. He had been looking for me. It was almost midnight and he explained that the city had been in turmoil all day and that we need to get out of town. He drove me back to Nashville. We stopped in North Birmingham, and I called Alma from a pay phone to let her know I was alright. It was so nice to hear her voice."

The men spent the next two ours catching up. Sam learned that after his graduation from Medical School, James and Alma had spent years in Washington D. C. and then New York City before finally returning home to Birmingham in 1983. James explained that he had concentrated his studies and practice on cancer because of Sam's stories of Joan's plight dealing with the disease. He also admitted to buying a few shares in Apple stock, remembering Sam's bizarre tales of phones and computers. The return on his small investment had put all three of his kids through college and grad school.

Neither man could still explain their bizarre experience. James had never told anyone fearing he would have been committed to an insane asylum or at least have lost his medical license. He once told Alma he had a dream and shared some of the story but could never bring himself to unravel it all. He said that he just hoped he could live to see 2022 and that fate would bring them together again. While the entire episode remained a mystery, the men agreed to meet for lunch every Wednesday and savor their time together once again, each hoping their time travels would never occur again.

THE END

www.ingramcontent.com/pod-product-compliance
Lightning Source LLC
Chambersburg PA
CBHW070837030726
47504CB00005B/1131